THE HERON

GIORGIO BASSANI

THE HERON

Translated from the Italian by William Weaver

A HELEN AND KURT WOLFF BOOK

HARCOURT, BRACE & WORLD, INC. | NEW YORK

to Beppe Minerbi

Elle est retrouvée.
Quoi? L'éternité.

RIMBAUD

PART ONE

I

Not immediately, but climbing with some effort up from the bottomless pit of unconsciousness, Edgardo Limentani stretched his right arm toward the bedside table. In the darkness the little traveling alarm clock that Nives, his wife, had given him in Basel three years before, on his forty-second birthday, continued emitting its shrill, insistent, but discreet sound. He had to silence it. He drew back his arm, opened his eyes and turned, his side supported by his elbow, as he stretched out the left arm; and at the very moment when his fingertips reached the Jaeger's soft, already slightly worn doeskin to press the alarm button, he read the time, marked by the position of the phosphorescent spheres on the dial. It was four o'clock: the time that, the night before, he had decided to be wakened. If he wanted to reach Volano an hour before daylight, he reminded himself, he hadn't a minute to waste. With one thing and another, getting up, going to the bathroom, washing, shaving, dressing, gulping down some coffee, and so on, he wouldn't be able to get into his car before five.

Finally, when he had turned on the light, sat up in bed, and looked slowly around, he was seized with a sudden sense of dejection and was tempted to let the whole thing go, to stay home.

Perhaps it was because of the chill in the room or the too-weak light that fell from the central chandelier; in any case, this bedroom where he had slept since childhood, except for a brief period just after his marriage

3

and then, naturally, the year and a half in Switzerland, had never seemed so alien to him, so squalid. The dark wardrobe, tall, broad, potbellied (his mother had always called it the *armoire bombée*), which occupied a good part of the left wall; the heavy chest of drawers against the wall opposite, surmounted by a little oval mirror, so opaque that it was useless, even for tying his tie; the little mahogany-and-glass gun case, there at the rear, tiny, next to the beige, vertical outline of the valance; the chairs; the clothes-stand on casters, where, yesterday afternoon, his mother had laid out in full view his woolen underwear, complete with long pants (the rest of his hunting clothes, boots included, she had put in the next room, the bath); the various picture frames—his diploma, the photographs, chiefly of mountain scenes—hanging more or less everywhere on the walls: each piece of furniture, each object which his eye fell on now jarred him, irked him. It was as if he were seeing it for the first time; or, to be more precise, as if only now he were able to see some base aspect of it, disagreeable, absurd.

He yawned. He ran his hand over his cheeks and chin, rough with beard, then pushed aside the blankets, and thrust his legs out of the bed. From a chair he took the camel-colored wool robe, put it on over his pajamas, stuck his feet into his slippers, and a few moments later he was at the window, looking through the panes and the half-closed shutters, down into the courtyard.

There was almost nothing to be seen. The court was so deep in shadow that the well in the center could barely be distinguished. Still from the kitchen window of the Manzolis, the concierge and his wife, came a strip of intense white light: it was so bright that it

4

reached the top of the high wall opposite, toward Via Montebello, and touched the upper branches of the big climbing rosebush which, in summer, covered the wall almost completely. Gusts of sirocco stirred the branches, disheveled them. Dry and light, they moved in jerks, as if an electric shock ran through them at intervals. It wasn't raining: as long as this wind kept up, it wouldn't rain.

He turned to look toward the entrance. The door of the ground-floor apartment, occupied by the Manzoli family, had opened. From it came more light (much less bright than what filtered through the kitchen window): against it a bent, bundled-up form was immediately outlined.

Romeo is already up, he observed.

Attentive and immobile, he then followed all the concierge's movements. He saw the man come forward, approach the wrought-iron gate that shut off the courtyard from the portico, open one wing of it a crack, step outside, examine, above his head, the dark sky, and finally, evidently seeing his master, Romeo took off his cap and looked toward him.

He opened the double panes, flung the shutters wide (he was struck by a gust of damp, sticky, almost warm wind), then leaned out to fasten them to the wall.

He straightened up again.

"Good morning," he said, turning to the concierge. "Ask Imelde, if she's up, to make me some coffee, please."

"Are you going off anyway, Signor Avvocato?" the other man asked, in dialect, also speaking in a low, calm voice.

He nodded yes, then closed the outer panes. Moving

from the sill, he had just time to see Romeo take off his cap again. How long had the Manzolis been in service in this house? he wondered, going into the bath, distracted slightly, as he passed the glass gun case, by the quiet gleam of the guns' barrels through the crystal. And he calculated that, more or less, the Manzolis must have been with the family for something like forty years.

He took off his robe, hung it on the peg fixed at the top of the door, and let some hot water run in the basin, taking his shaving things from their leather case. Meanwhile he examined himself in the mirror.

That face was his; and yet, he stood there, staring at it, as if it, too, didn't belong to him, as if it were the face of another. Minutely, distrustfully, he checked every detail of it: the bald, convex forehead; the three horizontal, parallel lines that furrowed the brow almost from temple to temple; the blue, washed-out eyes; the sparse eyebrows, exaggeratedly arched, which gave his whole face a perennially hesitant and puzzled expression; the rather pronounced nose which was, however, handsome, aquiline, an aristocrat's; the heavy, protruding lips, slightly womanish; the chin deformed at the tip by a kind of hole, shaped like a comma; the brick-reddish color of the long, discontented cheeks, smudged by a beard so black it seemed bluish. How base and disagreeable his face was, too, he said to himself, how absurd it was! His mother had always insisted, naturally pleased by the fact, that it resembled the face of the former King Umberto. Perhaps. One thing was clear at least: if the socialist-communist tide continued to advance (and there was nobody in sight who could arrest it. De Gasperi? With that face of his?), all the owners

6

of farm properties of any size, and among such owners, inevitably, also themselves, the Limentanis, proprietors of an estate like La Montina, with nearly a thousand acres, would soon be forced to abdicate. Starting at the tip of his chin, he set about lathering his face. And as its lines gradually disappeared behind the soap, he began to feel again, even more heavily than before, the weight of the day of hunting that lay ahead of him.

He was the one who had forced it on himself. And why, after all? For what reason? Wouldn't he have done better to give up, once and for all, that idea of shooting from a hogshead in a blind? Take his cousin Ulderico Cavaglieri, for example: though he lived permanently at Codigoro, only a stone's throw, in other words, from the valley, though he was protected, as always, by the huge, patriarchal, Catholic family he had created in the past fifteen years or so, though he could afford to thumb his nose even at the communists now, as in the past he had done at the Fascists of the Salò Republic and the German SS: he nevertheless hadn't felt it opportune to wait so long. On the contrary. In '38, the autumn of '38, the moment the racial laws had gone into effect (Ulderico was just forty then; whereas he, Edgardo, now was forty-five): *halt,* Ulderico hadn't allowed them to take away his gun license! He had simply refrained from applying for its renewal. And in '45, then, on the eve of the Liberation, he had carefully avoided the mistake of asking for a new license.

He shaved with his habitual care; waiting for the tub to fill, he slipped off his pajama bottoms and went to sit on the toilet. To free his bowels: for some years he had had to strain a bit, in the morning; and when he didn't

7

succeed—either because he had eaten too much the evening before, or because he had got up too early—afterwards, all through the day, he was in a bad humor, he even suffered palpitations of the heart. As he might have foreseen, this was a bad morning. But still, he couldn't set out on a journey in this state! If he did, there was the risk of having to stop halfway, and without even finding, perhaps, facilities for washing up afterwards.

So he sat there, in the roar of the water which poured into the tub, keeping his eye on the level as it gradually rose. He was thinking about hunting in the valley: about what it had been like before the war, and about what it had probably become now. Before the war, he remembered, a gentleman from Ferrara, on Sunday, could go and shoot off his gun somewhere around Codigoro or Comacchio, one hundred per cent sure of a pleasant welcome and general respect. And more: from the practical point of view, sure of the organization of the day, everything carefully prearranged—and obviously it had always been like that, for centuries—so this same gentleman could move easily, linger there, refresh himself, find on the spot, in other words, anything he might need. But nowadays? To begin with, it was already taking a big risk to drive through the countryside today in an automobile (the same as in '19 and '20, when there were those whose windshields were smashed by a stone, flung by an unknown hand from behind a hedgerow), so if he insisted on showing himself around those parts, with a shotgun over his shoulder or not, what could he expect but grim looks, backs obstinately turned, or, even, open sneers of defiance? The days of smiles, of doffed hats, of bows, were over.

For everyone: including former victims of political and racial persecution.

He thought, too, as he had been thinking, inevitably, for several months now, about the nasty mishap that he himself, just last April at La Montina, had suffered that day he had had the bright idea of going there to see how the work of leveling the terrain was proceeding.

The whole thing had happened suddenly, without the slightest forewarning.

He could still see himself, seated on the edge of a ditch, alone in the midst of the endless fields, with at least thirty farm workers around him (familiar faces, most of them, known perhaps for years and years!), their hoes raised, ready to be brought down on his skull, as the men asked him for an immediate revision of the crop-sharing agreement. Then and there he had given in, naturally: and Galassi-Tarabini, the family lawyer, whom he had consulted the moment he was back in the city, had wholeheartedly approved his "stratagem." But then, as a result of the lawyer's subsequent advice to pay no attention to his given promise and, in fact, to report the threatened violence to the Codigoro police, since that time, he hadn't felt like setting foot at La Montina again (after that day, his manager, the book-keeper Prearo, had had to visit La Montina now and then, to go over the few figures necessary with the farm manager Benazzi), and also since 1939, the whole property, agricultural and urban real estate, of the late Leone Limentani was in the name of his daughter-in-law Nives Limentani, née Pimpinati, Catholic, Aryan, and at that time eight months pregnant, so the son Edgardo and the late Leone's widow Erminia Calabresi Limentani, the direct heirs, had to consider the thousand or so acres of the estate—if not perhaps the house in Via Mentana in Ferrara, in which, for better or worse, they still lived—definitively the property of another.

Except for Galassi-Tarabini and Prearo the book-keeper, obviously, he had never mentioned the incident at La Montina to anyone: neither to his mother nor to his wife. His mother, certainly—you only had to observe how serene she was—so far had heard nothing. But Nives? Was it possible that Prearo, with whom, for some while now, he noticed she conferred more and more frequently in the management office, hadn't already amply informed her about the whole thing? And as for the agricultural circles of Codigoro and thereabouts, at least as far as Pomposa—the proletarian agricultural circle, above all—they must have rushed straight to the local Labor Council to fill everyone's head with the story!

But precisely for this reason: if this is how the situation stood, why run a risk, he asked himself again, why the hell should he lay himself open? Was it worth encountering more trouble, perhaps even physical unpleasantness, just for the fun of firing a few cartridges?

What was more important, in other words: hunting, or . . .

Dissatisfied, he stood up, rejecting the idea of sitting there any longer ("It's useless, anyway," he grumbled). He leaned over the tub and turned off the faucets. In the meanwhile the room had filled, little by little, with a thick, tepid fog.

II

Standing still at the closed door, his hand on the latch, not yet lowering it, he wondered if he would manage to slip away without any fuss.

He had said good-by to his mother and his wife the previous evening immediately after supper, when he had left them in the dining room, knitting in silence before the half-spent embers in the fireplace. True, he hadn't been able to say good-by to Rory, his little girl, the previous evening, since he had come home from the Concordi club at nine, and by nine o'clock Rory had been asleep for at least an hour. Now, in any case, there was no sense in hesitating. If, to give Rory a kiss, he had to face a supplementary round of farewells with Nives, who occupied the double bedroom next to his and, on the opposite side, next to the child's (his mother's room was at the front of the house: sufficiently far and isolated, thank God!), no, no: he would gladly do without that kiss then.

He opened his door slowly.

Once outside, he switched on the light, turned to shut the door, then took a few cautious steps along the linoleum of the corridor. Though he was wearing low American army boots, whose soles had no nails, still he moved his feet with extreme circumspection. Normally he weighed about a hundred and seventy-five pounds. But today, bundled as he was in his hunting clothes, and laden with two guns, the Browning and his old Krupp "Three Rings," today, no doubt about it, he must weigh an extra fifty pounds. A simple creak forced by his weight from the parquet under the linoleum, and Nives, who had always been a light sleeper, would wake up and call him.

"'Dgardo!"

"Sssh," he said, instinctively.

He hadn't made the slightest sound, he was sure of that, but Nives, God knows how, had managed to hear him all the same. What a bore, he grumbled. If he didn't go into her room at once, she would surely start yelling: without giving the least thought to Rory.

"'Dgardo!" Nives was, in fact, already repeating, in her nasal, country-girl drawl.

He stuck his head into the room, which was in complete darkness.

"Sssh," he whispered. "What is it? Wait a moment."

He disliked going into his wife's room with his guns, the cartridge belt over his belly, and everything: with the Browning in its showy holster of light beige leather, especially since, despite all his announced program of strict economy, he had bought it last September at Gualandi's, the best gunsmith's in Bologna. So slowly, calculating each movement, he freed himself of the Browning, hanging it by its strap on the handle of the window opposite. He was about to do the same with the other shotgun. But, after all, he could show that to her, to Nives, he reflected. She had seen it in his hands for a long time, ever since the Codigoro days, when she was only his kept woman; so that, very probably, now she wouldn't even notice it. And there was also the fact that, to avoid problems of whatever sort (she might even have *that* in mind: she was fully capable of getting ideas at a time like this!), there was nothing better than to give her the immediate impression that he was on his way, that he didn't have a single minute for chatting or anything else.

He went in.

Nives was turning on the lamp on the bedside table. With the thumb of his right hand between the gun's leather strap and the soft Scotch wool of his jacket, he moved toward the center of the room. And then, as he approached the great double bed with its carved headboard of reddish wood, where he, an only child, had been conceived, and where, since '39, he had slept so rarely with his wife, for the second time that morning he felt himself overcome by a strange feeling of absurdity. Yes: once again it was as if, between him and the things he saw, a thin, transparent sheet of glass were raised. The objects were all on the other side; and he, on this side, looked at them, one by one, amazed by them.

Nives yawned. Lazily she raised her bare arm, covered her mouth with the back of her hand. Half buried in the fat, waxy flesh of her palm, the narrow gold wedding ring could hardly be discerned.

"What time is it?" she asked at last.

"It must be about twenty minutes to five," he answered, looking at her face. "I have to go."

"My God, it must be cold out! Is it cold?"

"No, not very. I think it's going to rain."

"Take your raincoat with you, eh, 'Dgardo?"

"It's already down in the car."

"And the high boots. The rubber ones?"

"They're there, too."

They looked at each other as they talked: he, with his hands on the railing of the bed, Nives lying as always in her place, on the right side. But what they said to each other, obviously, had no importance. It served, for her too, merely to gain time. And she too, meanwhile, was examining, studying, investigating.

"I simply can't see how anybody could enjoy going hunting in the winter," Nives continued. "These days between Christmas and New Year's, especially! I bet you'll come home with pneumonia. Am I right?"

"No, no, why should I? It's just a question of keeping covered up."

"Have you put on your woolen underwear at least?"

"Yes, Mamma thought of that; she laid it out for me on the clothes-stand."

He absolutely hadn't meant anything by that remark, he could swear to it. Still Nives made a face.

"Since Mamma Erminia always wants to take care of you," she said, giving little vertical shakes to her head full of curlers, "it didn't seem polite for me to prevent her."

Thank God, she promptly changed her tone.

"How can you bear," she went on, "standing in the water for five or six hours on end? My God, you ought to remember at least that you're not a young man any more! I get the shivers just thinking about it. Brrr."

She laughed, blinking her little gray, inexpressive eyes; and from the foot of the bed, as he curiously observed their shape, and the shape of the nose beneath them, short and hooked like a bird of prey's, and then the mouth, with the thin upper lip, almost invisible, and the lower lip thick and protruding (a mouth seen from below—he said to himself—an upturned mouth), he felt wonderment growing within him. He was well aware how this little village woman between thirty and forty had happened to become his wife: oh, he was aware, all right! But at the same time, seeing her demurely play her role as lady of the highest society of the city, as if she had never set foot in the country, and especially in the Po plain, he couldn't believe it was true. Nives. La Nives. What was her real name? Her family name? Ah, of course: Pimpinati. Nives Pimpinati, now Limentani.

"What time will you be coming back this evening?"

"Oh, sometime after five."

"Will you also go and see *your* cousin?"

There was nothing strange, after all, about her asking him a question of the sort. It was surely no secret that he, after almost ten years had gone by, had finally decided to resume relations with Ulderico (only by telephone, true, and with the pretext of asking Ulderico to give him the name of somebody to take him in a boat through the valleys: but the ice, in any event, had been broken). Still, that question must have seemed to her in some way risky, indiscreet. She acted indifferent, but he knew her: there was no telling what was going on in her head. Poor Ulderico: she probably still couldn't forgive him for having done everything, in '39, to persuade him not to marry her. . . .

"I don't know," he answered. "Perhaps."

"What about eating? Where will you go to eat?"

"I don't know. At Caneviè perhaps. . . . Or maybe at Codigoro, at the usual *Bosco Eliceo*. There's not all that much choice."

Nives wrinkled her nose.

"At that old Fascist's, Bellagamba's?" she exclaimed. "That crackpot rat? I don't want to interfere, but rather than go there, I think you'd be better off eating at our own place, in the country. You could ask Benazzi's wife to fix you something: some spaghetti, a piece of meat . . . After all," she went on, the expression of her eyes hardening, and speaking, now, as if the question concerned her directly, "after all, La Montina still belongs to us, if I'm not mistaken!"

What was Nives getting at?

"Yes, I know I could just as well go there," he answered, ill at ease, looking away. "But if I arrive at three, or half past, or at four, which could easily happen, it would mean too much trouble. For everybody. I prefer just to stop off somewhere and eat. I'll find a place!"

"As you like," Nives agreed. She smiled, pursing her lips. "After all, you're the one," she continued, "who must decide. But you know what I think? I'd like to have the satisfaction of going there, to La Montina, every now and then, perhaps making somebody take me. I can accept anything, but what with having scruples, and not wanting to cause trouble, little by little *they* end up owning it, our land. And with everything on their side: you want to wait and see?"

It had to be one thing or the other: either she didn't know what had happened to him last April at La Montina, and in this case, her *"they"* (as she said it—he had noticed—her lips made a circumflex accent) had been meant to refer, generically, to the thousands and thousands of Pimpinatis, Benazzis, Callegaris, Callegarinis, Patrignanis, Tagliatis, et cetera, "agitating" for more than a year, on all the big estates of the Ferrara plain, from the gates of the city to the sea, to get more, and then still more, from the owners. Or else, on the con-

16

trary, she did know: and then she was inviting him to speak, to abandon his reserve, to confide in her.

This latter prospect filled him, all of a sudden, with a kind of fear. Confide in Nives! And to tell her what, after all?

"You know what Prearo told me last evening?" Nives went on, in the meanwhile. "He said . . ."

"That's not the reason," he interrupted her. "It's because I don't want to drive an extra ten miles in the car. And besides, if it rains, I'd risk getting stuck in the mud."

He moved brusquely from the bed, turning his back to her.

"If you start home after five," Nives shouted after him, "watch out for the fog, eh?"

"All right, of course, I know."

Since she had been sleeping there alone, she had reorganized the room. On the night table, in addition to the image of Santa Maria Ausiliatrice, to whom the main church of Codigoro, the one in the square, was dedicated, she had also set a little radio, a basket with sewing things, photographs of her parents, and a deck of playing cards. Why did they go on living together? he asked himself, leaving the room. Why didn't they separate finally?

In front of the Browning, in the corridor, he stood still for a moment, again undecided what to do. He checked the time by the Vacheron-Constantin on his wrist, gold (another souvenir of Switzerland): four fifty-eight. It was late, he said to himself, late, but nevertheless . . . And immediately, instead of burdening himself with the second gun, he took a flashlight from his pocket and moved toward the door of his daughter's bedroom.

He turned out the light in the hall, clicked on the flashlight, pressed down the door handle, and stepped softly into the room. Separate, yes, he thought, tiptoeing in the vague odor of talcum powder, schoolbooks, chalk, and floor wax which wafted among those walls. It was easy to say it, separate. But, practically speaking, how could they arrive at a separation? How much would it cost, in lawyers' fees? No small amount, obviously. And, in that case, how would it be possible for him, who now owned nothing, to collect the necessary sum? "After all, La Montina still belongs to us, if I'm not mistaken," Nives had said a moment before, emphasizing the "us" and the "mistaken." She really couldn't have found a more effective turn of phrase, to remind him how things actually stood.

But apart from that, what about Rory?

When he reached the little bed, he stopped. Almost without breathing, with his heart beating, and he could feel it, grimly in his throat, he turned the beam of light first on the miniature Christmas tree, set, in a pot, beside the head of the bed, and then, on the little body lying under the soft blanket of pink angora wool: beginning with the tiny swell of the feet, and then moving up, up to the shoulder and the lower part of the cheek. And as he gazed at her, at Rory, surprised, as always, by how beautiful she was, how alive, how strong (yes, yes, that face did perhaps resemble his slightly, especially the eyes—though hers were big, they were huge! —and the line of the lips), suddenly he was oppressed by an ineffable anguish, by a desolation beyond all remedy. He didn't know why. It was as if someone, unexpectedly and in silence, had flung himself on him. As if he had been assailed by a wild animal.

He bent to graze the child's forehead with his lips, then crossed the room again, and went out into the hall for the third time. He pressed the light switch and looked at the time. Five past five. He went back to take the gun from the window handle, hung it over his left shoulder, and started out. And in a little while, with the sensation of lowering himself into a well, he went slowly down the dark, spiral staircase that led below, to the entrance portico.

III

It was very cold, down in the portico: a damp, insidious cold, really like a well, like a cellar. Bursting in gusts through the big door to the street which Romeo, for some unknown reason, had already flung wide open, the wind made the little black wrought-iron lamp sway perilously, as it hung high above from the coffered, shadowy ceiling.

The concierge was motionless, there in the background, at the main gate, intent, or so it seemed, on looking out, toward the invisible façade of the house opposite. He stopped to peer at Romeo, uneasily. What was he looking there for? With his bent, slightly humped back, obstinately turned away, like a striking worker's, he seemed not only not to have noticed the other man's presence, but even to have forgotten that, before leaving, he still had to drink his coffee and that always, in any case, especially in winter, he was accustomed to allow the motor to warm up, without the slightest haste.

Melancholy, trusted, familiar shape, his old dark blue Aprilia was waiting in the center of the portico, its nose turned toward the gate to the courtyard, left ajar. He walked around the automobile, and laid the guns on the bench against the wall opposite the stairs, then he retraced his steps, opened the right-hand door, and sat at the wheel. As he fiddled with the starter (he had trouble starting the motor: because of the cold, no doubt, but also the battery, too old, like all the rest), he didn't take his eyes off the immobile, enigmatic sight of Romeo reflected in the rear-view mirror. During the almost thirty years that the man had witnessed these early-morning departures for the country, never, he said to himself, never had Romeo behaved like this before. What was it? Was he annoyed, all of a sudden, at having been forced, as in the old days, to get up before dawn, and on a Sunday? Was this what Romeo wanted him to realize? With the present situation, anything was possible; this, in any event, was a novelty, and not an especially pleasant one.

After a few coughs, the motor finally started. With some effort, because of the cartridge belt around his waist, he bent forward to hunt for the knob of the choke, under the dashboard. When he sat up again, he was surprised to find himself face to face with Romeo. The man stood there, beside the door, bent in a slight bow, and looking at him from beneath those heavy eyelids, like an old tortoise's.

"Would you like to come and have your coffee?" he asked softly, in dialect.

He knew the concierge's character well: brusque, cross at times, perhaps, he was still affectionate and of proven loyalty. And now, he said to himself, and his chest swelled with relief, now it was quite clear that Romeo was not cherishing the slightest resentment toward him. And what's more, he could sense from the vaguely humorous expression which played over the older man's cheekbones, impassive as always, that Romeo was, on the contrary, happy, secretly pleased and satisfied at seeing his master going hunting again, after so many years.

He got out of the car, grumbling: "Is it ready?"

Romeo nodded. Then, pointing his chin toward the two guns, he asked if he should place them in the back, in the trunk.

"If you'll give me the keys," he said, "I'll put both of them in the trunk."

"No, it doesn't matter," he answered, taking care to maintain the tone of cool reserve which always, since his childhood, had characterized their relationship. "You'd better put them on the back seat. This too, if you don't mind."

He freed himself of the cartridge belt, lay it, outstretched, on the concierge's arms, after which, with rapid steps, he went toward the illuminated fissure of the Manzolis' door.

The apartment where they lived consisted of three communicating rooms, in line, one after the other. At one end there was the kitchen, which looked out over the courtyard; at the opposite end, the double bedroom, with a window on Via Mentana; in between, a huge room which the two old people, since their daughter, Irma, had gone to live with her husband, had filled with shiny, factory-made furniture but where, in practice, they never sat. As always, since the incident of last April at La Montina, this time too, when he stepped into the lodge—into the kitchen, especially: so neat, so clean, so well lighted, and, above all, so well heated by the glowing tiles of the cheap stove—his morale abruptly lifted. Here, he exclaimed again, within himself, now reassured—here, indeed, he felt at his ease, truly and completely at home. The Manzolis were trustworthy people, all right!

He sat at the table and began to sip slowly the steaming coffee from the bowl without a handle which was always reserved for him, his *"mastèla dal caffè,"* his coffee pail, as it was called by Romeo, who, for his part —a while back he had been led to say explicitly— would have liked to live on coffee alone. Meanwhile Imelde, her sharp face hidden in the folds of the peasant housewife's black kerchief, bustled about the room.

He stared at her, over the curved brim of the big cup, following intently her every movement.

Neither she nor Romeo could stand Nives. More or less openly, they disapproved of everything about her, involving in the same disapproval Prearo the bookkeeper, Elsa the cook, and even Rory: every person and thing that had come to number 2 Via Mentana *after* '38, in short. When they spoke to him about her, they never mentioned her by name. They referred to her regularly as *"your* Signora," since the only true Signora, the real lady of the house, remained, for them, Signora Erminia, and Lilla, the three-year-old poodle that kept his mother company even in bed, remained the sole, true baby to coddle and spoil in every way. Nothing Nives did was ever right, for them. If he stepped into their quarters even for a moment, Romeo or his wife would promptly begin the usual complaints.

Recently, for example, they had reported to him Nives's habit, when he wasn't at home, of systematically ignoring the house telephone. For the slightest errand, either she or Elsa would lean from the windows on the courtyard and let out shouts and screams the like of which were never heard even in the courtyard of the Palazzone, the slum in Via Mortara. . . . What now? he wondered, lowering his eyelids, as if, with this, it were easier for him to draw on that infinite source of patience he knew he possessed. Now what would he have to listen to, against his wife? Imelde was surely brooding over something.

He raised his eyelids again.

"What is it?" he said.

Again he was mistaken, however; again it was nothing like what he had imagined. Imelde's eyes were red, and she kept putting her handkerchief to her nose and, shaking her head, couldn't bring herself to speak. But then: as soon as Romeo came in from the portico, she began to curse against William, "that good-for-nothing, that communist of a William" who—she said—though he had qualified as a skilled electrician, refused to work, spent all his money at the brothel, and lived, he and his wife, practically on their money, poor old people.

He turned toward Romeo.

"Who is this William?" he asked.

"Irma's husband," Romeo answered, bluntly, bending his silvery head under the light.

For a moment he didn't understand: as if his memory, defending his peace of mind, refused to serve him. But then he remembered.

Of course, he said to himself, Irma's husband, their daughter. How could he have forgotten?

William was a young man of about twenty-five, he recalled, slim, blond, an easy talker, well-mannered: a character who until a short time ago he often ran across, moving around the portico or the courtyard, and who even, once, had not only offered to wash the car but, after having done the job, had refused any payment for it. Communist? He might very well be one: you only had to look at him, and the suspicion arose spontaneously: that thin, pale face, greedy, riven by se-

24

cret resentments; you had only to hear him expressing himself in his radio-announcer's Italian: smooth and fluent, true, but also treacherous. And the only amazing thing was how Irma, of all people, such a meek girl, and so refined, brought up as she had been at the nuns' sewing school on Via Borgo di Sotto, and ready to turn bright red if a man, far from accosting her, simply crossed her path or said hello—how could she have become spellbound by an individual of that sort?

Now Irma was pregnant, Imelde was explaining to him, six months pregnant. And she was the one, working from morning to night, doing mending, to pay for the vices of her good-for-nothing husband. . . .

He felt his uneasiness growing, and yet he stayed there, he still couldn't make up his mind to go. He looked at the time: five thirty-five. Ulderico, on the phone, had been precise: the man he had found, who was to take him with the boat from the Lungari di Rottagrande to the blind (his name was Gavino, if he had heard it right), would wait for him at Volano, opposite the Tuffanelli hunting lodge, from quarter past six on. Five thirty-five. There was no hope of his meeting this Gavino by quarter past six. He would reach there at six thirty at best, or six forty-five. To say nothing of the fact that, as he remembered it, to go then from the Tuffanelli lodge to the Lungari di Rottagrande, you had to drive around Valle Nuova for about a third of its perimeter, and so it took, with one thing and another, a good half-hour extra. In other words: if all went well, he would take his position in the hogshead no earlier than quarter past seven, or half past: when the sun was already up. And even then, only if he left now, at once.

He looked at his watch, trying to hurry himself, to

find the strength necessary to stand up. It was no good: an immense laziness, stronger than any demand on his will, kept him seated in the rush-bottom chair of the Manzoli kitchen, as if he were tied to it. Oh, if he could have stayed there, despite everything, in the warmth of the concierge's lodge, hidden from his family and from everyone else, until evening! He would have given anything in exchange.

He raised his face toward Imelde.

"But, after all," he said to her, "what's the reason why your son-in-law doesn't want to work?"

Shrugging her thin shoulders, Imelde answered that she didn't know. "How should I know?" she said. She knew only one thing, she went on—that her son-in-law stayed in bed all day, and if she, Irma, ever tried to scold him, "to give him what for," that crook, that communist, was even capable of hitting her.

It was true. They swore to him it was true, Romeo's face, livid with ill-repressed bitterness, and hers, even more, with those eyes, like the eyes of a foreordained victim, perhaps a willing one.

Confused, he started to get up.

"If he isn't working," he tried to rebut, "it must be because he hasn't found anything to do."

Romeo spoke up.

"Oh no, no," he said, shaking his head. "He just doesn't feel like doing anything at all."

"But if that's so," he insisted, again addressing Imelde, "why don't you have your daughter come back here, to stay with you?"

The woman sighed. She had suggested it to Irma again and again, she said, but Irma has a hard head, "harder than a rock." She wouldn't even hear of it.

"She's in love," she said finally, twisting her thin lips in a grimace of contempt.

In love, of course: as he had already realized, for that matter. And now the Manzoli kitchen, too, had abruptly become uninhabitable: this, too, a place from which he had to clear out. And at once.

In the silence after Imelde's last words (through the walls he could hear only, from the portico, the muffled grumbling of the Aprilia's engine), he looked again at his watch. Five fifty-two.

"Well, I must be off," he said.

He gripped the edge of the table with both hands, pulled himself to his feet, and started to go. And to Imelde, who followed him, begging him to do something for Irma (if he would just send for her son-in-law, she said, and talk to him—who knows?—that wretch might finally decide to change his ways!), he answered with a "We'll see," which, as he was the first to know, hadn't the slightest meaning.

Send for that character? he said to himself, in fact, as he went out into the portico and headed for the car. Speak to him? Imagining himself in conversation with the young electrician with the cadaverous face, he felt a kind of disgust. Disgust mixed with fear.

He climbed into the car. He turned on the headlights. He backed out of the portico. Finally, waving in response to the respectful good-by from Romeo, who had followed him at every step into the street, and now, standing at the sidewalk, stared at him in silence, with the weak light of the entrance behind him, he shifted gears and drove off.

IV

He couldn't wait to put Codigoro behind him.

For a good part of the trip, from the arches at the end of Corso Giovecca to the outskirts of Codigoro, he had driven with his eyes fixed constantly on the road. At Volano, the man with the boat was already waiting, so he had to hurry. But, in addition to that, it was only after Codigoro, after Pomposa, when he would see, in the uncertain light of dawn, the landscape of the low, deserted terrain take shape, broken by expanses of apparently stagnant water which was, really, flowing, linked as they were with the open sea, only then, he felt, would he be really at ease, able to breathe.

But, just at the outskirts of Codigoro, perhaps a hundred yards before he was to turn off the smooth ring road, a sharp pain, at the level of his belt, heralded, a moment before, by a slight palpitation of the heart, forced him to bend abruptly over the wheel.

This is it, thank God, he grumbled, glancing up, through the windshield, at the two identical, looming towers of the Eridania sugar refinery, and the other tower, farther on, of the pump of the Reclamation Bureau.

He knew the workings of his body. He could hold out for a maximum of ten minutes, no more. Would that be enough?

He took advantage of the first, widely spaced city lights, swaying madly above the rough cobbles of the village, to look at his watch. Six forty. At that hour the

28

two cafés in the square would surely have pulled up their metal shutters. Better then, more reasonable, to give up the idea of continuing directly to Volano, and to stop here, at Codigoro. If he could make the square (a matter of two minutes), he could consider himself safe.

Continuing in a straight line, in a few moments he reached the center of the town and came into the square. No lights—he saw at once: irritated, yes, but also, absurdly, feeling a faint relief—either from the two cafés, one opposite the other, or from the ten-story I.N.A. building, on the other side, where Ulderico and his family lived, or from the other buildings or houses around. Everything was closed, dark. Not a soul.

He brought the car to a stop on the left, against the big modern building, the former Casa del Fascio, now a carabiniere barracks. He turned off the engine, the headlights, and stepped out, calmly locking the door. Codigoro. The square of Codigoro. For about ten years, since '38, he hadn't been there at such an early hour. But, all the same, he couldn't recall ever having seen it so deserted. What could have caused this emptiness? Was it, he snickered, the communist terror? Or simply the Christmas season?

It wasn't cold; and, at least in this spot, there was hardly any wind blowing. Strange: even his belly had stopped hurting. A dog came from the shadows that filled the arcade at the base of the I.N.A. building: a pointer, judging by its trot. He saw the dog come into the open, toward the center of the square (it was, in fact, an old pointer), encountering in its path the Monument to the Dead of the First World War, sniffing its base thoroughly, peeing on it, finally, still at a trot, disappearing to the right, into an alley. What if he were to try Bellagamba's? he asked himself, alone again. Perhaps not even the *Bosco Elìceo* was open, true. But if worst came to worst, since, after all, it was a hotel (he had never slept there: but there were surely rooms, upstairs; he had heard them mentioned more than once), if worst came to worst, he could ring the bell.

He opened the trunk, took out a gray astrakhan cap, Russian style (an old head-covering he had always used, even as a young man, both for hunting in the plain and, in the mountains, for skiing), pulled it on his head; then, moving about twenty yards from the car, he reached the former Casa del Fascio, the corner of the street flanking it. He looked, sharpening his gaze. He had been right: the *Bosco Elìceo* was also closed. Well, he said to himself, he would have to ring the bell. Since he had to stop somehow, he had no other choice.

And yet, when he was there, outside the lowered shutter, with the neon sign sputtering over his head, the sudden thought of facing Bellagamba, who, for that matter, might not even come down to open the door, was enough to make him hesitate.

He remembered Bellagamba in '38 and '39, in his uniform as Corporal of Militia (his name was Gino, he thought: Gino Bellagamba), with the fez thrust back on his shaved neck, and the black tassel hanging halfway down his bull's back; he remembered his villainous expression then, a country braggart called back to active service by the events; how he stood almost permanently in the square, like a mastiff on guard, outside the Casa del Fascio, on the sidewalk; the menacing and contemptuous glances which even he, as a "Hebrew," as a "nonpolitical," and as a landowner, had abundantly received on the rare occasions when, driving out to Codigoro because of La Montina, he had been unlucky enough to come within range. No, he said to himself, to have to face that mug again, with whom, for that matter, he had never exchanged a word in his whole life, and to ask him what he had to ask, namely permission to use his bathroom: all this would not be pleasant, not at all. He would even, if it had been just a little later, he would even have preferred to do an about-face and go ring the doorbell of the Cavaglieris' house.

But still, what else could he find? And then, frankly, was it worth all the difficulties he was creating for himself? He had always avoided applying for a Fascist party card (not because he had ever been *anti*, really, but just because, because of a certain unsociable side of his character): in this, he had behaved differently from Ulderico, in any case, who, for his part, when they had offered him the card in '32, hadn't waited to be asked twice: he had pocketed it immediately. However, when you came right down to it, were they really so much worse, those Fascists before '43, than the communists now? And the Labor Councils today, as centers of tyranny set up against the landowners, were they perhaps better than the Casa del Fascio and the Fascist Neighborhood Cells of the past? As for Bellagamba, it may be true, as Nives insisted, that after the Badoglio period he joined up with the Salò crowd. Quite possible. In any case, if even the communists, who today were the undisputed masters of Codigoro, left him alone and allowed him to prosper, why should he, Edgardo Limentani, of all people, make any fuss? Anyway he knew that Nives had a single mania: to attack the people of her native town. And any opportunity was good enough for her. . . .

While he stood there, hesitant, and moreover uneasy about the fate of the two guns left in plain sight on the rear seat of the car (perhaps it would be better to go back at once and stick them too, with the cartridge belt, in the trunk), at a certain point he thought he heard some noises inside the building. They were sighs, puffs, moans, creaks: as if produced by someone laboriously shifting furniture.

He waited for a while, in silence, then he rapped his knuckles discreetly against the corrugated metal.

He was assailed by a violent voice, wrathful and frightened at the same time.

"Who's there?"

"Friend," he answered, softly.

"What friend?"

He hesitated. Beyond the shutter he heard heavy footsteps approach, then stop. He said: "Limentani."

"Who?"

"Li-men-ta-ni," he repeated, not raising his voice, amazed, all of a sudden, at his own last name, at the way the syllables of his own name resounded in the open air.

With a single yank, the shutter was rolled up entirely.

It was really Bellagamba, he saw, even heavier, fatter, more bull-like than in the past: with his chest, beneath his undershirt, rounded like a woman's. And, gripped again by his old repugnance, he was about to turn his back and go off. Perhaps he was still in time.

But it was too late, the man was already widening his pale blue eyes: he had recognized him.

"Well, well," he exclaimed, in a low voice.

He smiled, proud of himself, showing his tight, little boxer's teeth.

"Well, well," he said. "You know, Signor Avvocato," he went on, still whispering—and meanwhile, as he stepped aside, he winked with an air of complicity—"you know, you almost scared me? Come in, come, make yourself at home. It's cold out there. Come inside!"

He would have expected anything but this cordial, garrulous welcome (strange: Bellagamba too, like that William, Irma Manzoli's husband, spoke an unusually fluent, easy, polished Italian). In any case, he wasn't pleased by it. He would almost prefer to have been received badly, with hostility, so that it would, if anything, be up to him to be generous, casual, the perfect gentleman. What did this conspiratorial manner of Bellagamba's mean? Was he, this character, by any chance calculating that having once lured him into his den, he would then induce him to sigh, with him, over the golden age of the Empire, or even the great days of the Salò Republic? Bellagamba, too, surely, like everyone in Codigoro, knew all about what had happened at La Montina last April. But if he thought for a moment, now, that he would receive confidences and unburdenings, then the man was sorely mistaken. He bore no grudge against anyone in the world, and least of all against Bellagamba. But one thing was sure: the man wasn't going to be encouraged.

Meanwhile he had gone inside: with the impression, the distinct sensation, also because of the very strong smell of fried fish that had overwhelmed him the moment he crossed the threshold, that he was entering a cavern, the den of a wild animal. He took off his fur cap and looked around. He was in the center of a medium-sized room, immersed in almost complete darkness. From the wall opposite the entrance, on a kind of little isolated dais, a table lamp, shrouded in a green silk shade, cast a faint, yellowish light.

The dais, he realized at once, was simply the hotel clerk's *bureau:* brand-new. Behind it, from a double row of numbered hooks on the newly whitewashed wall hung ten or twelve keys. In the penumbra he could see nothing else. But that was enough. That desk and those keys were enough for him to realize how little the present place, transformed by the ex-Corporal of the Militia into restaurant and hotel, resembled the unpretentious country eating place of the past, as he remembered it.

Bellagamba had remained behind. He could hear him grumbling, muttering, cursing the shutter which refused to come down again. From time to time, in addition to this, he warned him to watch his step. On the floor there was a half-shattered packing case, with some heavy object inside: a scale, which had arrived the night before from Milan, with the bus. He might stumble, hurt himself.

Finally Bellagamba came back, passed in front of him, not without jostling him slightly and putting under his nose, as he grazed by, the odor of his armpits; he headed for the desk, turned a switch next to the keys. At last, in the insufficient glow of a big neon tube, set across the center of the ceiling, they stood face to face: he, seated on an imitation leather armchair, and Bellagamba, there, behind the desk, his broad jaw bisected by the yellow light of the table lamp.

With the sensation, stronger than ever, of being outside the world, he didn't know how to begin. To ask for something to drink was out of the question. He felt his stomach clenched like a fist.

It was Bellagamba, in any event, who came to his aid.

"But what are you doing," he inquired, in an insinuating tone, dropping suddenly into dialect, and half closing his pale, watery eyes, "what are you doing around here? Excuse my asking. Have you come to Codigoro to hunt?"

Seeing how he was dressed, the question was really superfluous. But asked in that tone, insinuating and humble at the same time—the same tone that, until a few years ago, would have been used, in addressing him, by a peasant on his lands—it was enough to restore to him a minimum of self-confidence.

He nodded.

Yes, he said then, he had come here precisely for that reason: to fire a few cartridges. But would he manage to fire them, in the end? he added, and he really doubted it, all of a sudden. He was too late, he went on, he should have been at Volano some time ago by now: six, quarter past six. And now (he raised his cuff with one finger, glanced at the watch), now it was already after seven.

Finally he made up his mind.

He stood up, glanced around.

"Could I use your bathroom for a moment?" he asked.

V

The stairs were ahead of him, steep and straight.

He went up slowly, one step after the other, holding the polished wooden railing, and staring, at the same time, toward the second-floor landing, watching it gradually approach. Above, from a kind of porthole which had been placed halfway up the rear wall, the sky appeared. It was a dark sky, with swollen, swift clouds running across it. Dawn was breaking.

When he stepped onto the landing, he stopped for a moment to catch his breath. On his left and on his right were two short corridors, dimly lighted, all the bedroom doors shut. Outside one door, the last on the corridor to the right, a solitary pair of man's shoes was waiting, set on the floor. . . .

He had really done things up in grand style, Bellagamba, he said to himself, looking at those shoes, he really hadn't heeded expense. But what was surprising about that? There was plenty of money around, after all, plenty. For everybody. The only ones who always got no for an answer, the only ones, now, cut off from the flow of bank loans, were those few old-fashioned landowners who still existed, hanging on by their teeth and their fingernails, some for one reason, some for another, clinging to the traditional wheat, the traditional hemp, the same sugar beets, and therefore, communism or not, soon destined to vanish, to be swept away. Yes, yes, all right: another man, in his place, would perhaps have listened to Nives and to Prearo, who for

36

some time had missed no opportunity to hint that it was time to quit, enough was enough, he had to make up his mind once and for all to give up the old traditional crops, which had become virtually a deficit operation, and turn himself, like so many others, like the majority, into a simple fruitgrower. Another, in his shoes, not giving a damn about communist threats, one fine day would turn up at La Montina with a nice escort of carabinieri, and would fire them all, beginning with that slippery Benazzi, the farm manager, down to the last of the laborers and the stableboys. Another man. But not he: he could see the banks were right, the Cassa Agricola of Ferrara included, ready to finance anybody at all, even a Bellagamba, but not certain "relics of the past," as he had happened to read even in progovernment papers like the *Giornale dell'Emilia*. He had only to think of himself, of himself as an agriculturist, and he promptly forgot any project of that sort, admitting that he had outlived his day.

Meanwhile he had climbed a second flight of steps. Broken by a half-landing, these were much less tiring than the first. He started up a third, steep again. Finally, never taking his eyes off another porthole, like the one below, he reached the top, the last floor.

Here, too, the same empty, half-dark corridors, the same closed doors. Somewhat to the right of the stairwell, he immediately recognized the door he was looking for. Bellagamba, a short while before, had been explicit: "It's written on the door, too, you'll see," he had said, directing him at all costs, as if he wanted to put his best foot forward, not to the "water closet" on the ground floor, but to the one which he evidently considered the only bathroom in the hotel worthy of receiving a distinguished guest. In fact, so it was. The door, straw-colored, bore, at three-quarters of its height, an enam-eled metal plate on which he read: BATH. It looked like a miniature street sign, he thought, the kind they used in the past, before the other war, today scarcer than hen's teeth. The blue of the capital letters, narrow and elongated, and of the thin line that framed them, was the same: a deep blue, almost black.

He went inside.

Even before he turned on the light he realized that the bath was really a bathroom: complete, that is, not only with toilet, a basin surmounted by a mirror, but also a bidet with two faucets and a rectangular cast-iron tub.

The toilet was placed beyond the tub, by the window. He went over; he examined the seat: its wood, blondish in color, retained ancient traces of white paint. He raised it with his foot. Then, removing his jacket and his cap, which he hung from the window handle, he unbuttoned his trousers and his two pairs of under-pants, lowered them, and sat down, in direct contact with the chilly porcelain.

But nothing, again, nothing happened: his abdomen would have no part of emptying itself for him. Despite every effort, he felt he wouldn't make it this time either, or at most, the results would be scant.

On the window's low sill, perhaps three feet from his forearm, there was some newspaper: a little pile of rec-tangular scraps, all alike, which a sea pebble, dark and porous, held fast and in order. He reached out his hand, slipping the first piece of paper on the pile from under the stone. It must have been part of a newspaper of some months ago, he reflected, considering the yellowish color of the paper, perhaps an old issue of the *Giornale dell'Emilia*. ASPERI IN NEW YORK, a headline said, in big letters. Now then, he tried to recall, when had De Gasperi gone to America, to talk with Truman and Marshall? Was it April? Or May? Or even before? Before, it must have been earlier. The communists had been expelled from the cabinet only *after* the crisis of last May. And the crisis, the last in a series, had blown up (this he remembered exactly) when De Gasperi had been back in Italy for some while. In January, then? February?

He took various other slips of paper, at random; he was unable to establish the origin of any of them, but not all were cut from the pages of the same paper, and not all were of the same date. IGHT TO REBELLI—ATED BY CONSTI, another headline said, in letters even bigger than the first. And another: OGLIATTI AND NENNI— ATTACK GOVERNME; and another still: VE JEWISH BLOOD—IN TODAY'S POLAND.

He tried to read a bit of the article that followed, over two columns, under this last headline.

It was a report from Cracow. According to the author of the article, one was to believe that in Red Poland, in 1947, the persecution of the Jews continued and was no less cruel and bloody than in the brownshirt Poland of Gauleiter Frank, Hitler's governor general. Was it possible? The article's tone seemed excessively vehement. The man who had written it was undoubtedly exaggerating. But at the bottom of it, nevertheless, there must be some truth. My God, he grimaced, it couldn't be all lies!

He raised his head and allowed his thoughts to wander, as he looked out of the window. Dark, but limpid, the daylight was now full. No fog, no mist. Below the window, adjoining, or almost, the dirty little courtyard where Bellagamba kept his hens, he could see, in vertical perspective, the expanse of a bare, wretched football field, with its lonely goal posts at the two ends, of which, even at this distance, he thought he could perceive all the gray, fragile, worm-eaten decrepitude. Beyond the playing field, the whole town, practically: the dark tiles of its roofs, so different from those of the Ferrara roofs (heavier, more irregular: they might even have been made by hand, one by one), but also so similar, so obviously of the same family. And there, to one side, the central square, the Church of Santa Maria Ausiliatrice at one end, at the other the red façade of the Labor Council between the now-lighted windows of the two cafés, and in the middle, almost on the same line, far taller than the roofs of the modest, low, private houses, the two massive bulks, the former Casa del Fascio and the I.N.A. building, facing each other. And then, farther on, the inlet of the river port, hidden, yes, between the two shores, but precisely identifiable by the freight barges' masts which rose from the dock. And finally, still farther away, much farther, along the paved ribbon of the Ferrara highway, tall, against the rows of numbed poplars that marked, this side of the Volano Po, the northern boundary of La Montina, the slender, smoke-blackened chimneys of the Eridania sugar refinery, and the other, lower tower of the Reclamation Bureau's pump. . . . Like a surveyor without his necessary instruments, he tried to measure distances and proportions with his naked eye. How far, in a straight line, he wondered, idly, without trying to calculate it—how far, in a straight line, was the square from the river port? And the group of chimneys, down there to the right, how far was it from the ancient, dark, half-ruined watchtower, the Torre del Gallo, tiny, in the midst of the bare terrain of La Montina: just a bit more visible than the peasant farmhouses scattered at great intervals through the property? Try as he might, he couldn't make out the little villa (sold later, at the time of the racial laws) where, back in '30, he had installed Nives, and where, for years, he had entered as lord and master, no, he couldn't see it. Isolated, in those days, at the southern edge of the town, today it couldn't be distinguished among so many others which had sprung up, afterwards, in the area, all more or less in the same style. But it didn't matter: how many hundreds of yards separated that neighborhood, still the most modern part of Codigoro, from the central square? And the ash-colored statue of the infantryman who, on top of the Monument to the Dead, in the square, flung himself into the attack, waving over his helmet the tattered, bullet-ridden flag of his regiment: was he smaller or larger than life size?

The course of his reflections shifted again. He thought of Ulderico now, his cousin, his friend, his great friend, the inseparable companion of the first thirty years of his life (it seemed incredible to him, suddenly, that in the fifteen following years the two of them could have become such strangers), who, for fifteen years, in fact, after having rented the house in Via Montebello, in Ferrara, to the Reclamation Bureau, had come to live in Codigoro, a stone's throw from his land, and not in a handsome villa with a park on the outskirts, but in a commonplace apartment, large, comfortable, but commonplace, right in the center of the town. And thinking of Ulderico, and of himself, and of their lives, so similar and so different, at a certain point he decided that this afternoon, later, before going back to Ferrara, provided he didn't feel too tired and had some game to take as a present (in the dark, moreover, and the then inevitable fog, the chances of being noticed, of having unpleasant encounters in the street, could be considered practically nonexistent), today he would surely go to visit them, the Cavaglieri family: Ulderico, his wife Cesarina, and all the offspring. True, so far he hadn't been in their house even once: neither before the war, nor during it, and still less in the past three years, since his return from Switzerland. Of the children—six!—he hadn't yet seen even one. But after the two phone calls he and Ulderico had exchanged last week; after all his cousin's lavish kindness, and not least, his kindness in showing no surprise, on the phone, hearing his voice again: what would be the sense, for either of them, to go on stubbornly not seeing each other? How odd life was. He remembered the enormous scandal in '32, in the family and outside it, when Ulderico, abruptly, decided to marry, in church, Cesarina, the trouser-maker of Codigoro (and what the devil was her family name?), with whom for the longest time he had been carrying on an affair that could have been considered public, and, on top of it all, to have himself baptized on the day of his marriage. And he remembered, on the contrary, Ulderico's equal insistence, his sudden and unbearable interference, his absurd, by then ill-timed determination, in '39, that he should give up the idea of marrying, in his turn, his own kept mistress, Nives. . . .

No, he concluded, no: to continue not seeing each other, to avoid each other obstinately as if from fear, none of this, now, could have the slightest meaning.

VI

Later, when he went downstairs, he couldn't find Bellagamba. He congratulated himself on his luck. To exchange farewells with the ex-Corporal of Militia: what a bore that would have been, what a nuisance. He wanted only to slip away, to leave Codigoro behind as quickly as possible.

But, a moment later, as soon as he stepped into the square, he saw the man, it was Bellagamba all right, standing at the edge of the same sidewalk from which, in the old days, he had hurled inquisitorial glances at all, townspeople and outsiders (now standing by the Aprilia, his own old Aprilia, one foot placed against a front tire, he seemed to be making a connoisseur's evaluation of the car's condition), he realized that it wouldn't be possible to evade the man, and that he would have to resign himself to losing more time.

Approaching, he observed him. He was almost unrecognizable. Over a high-necked, cyclist's jersey, iron-gray in color, he was wearing a dark, double-breasted overcoat; on his head he wore a soft hat, its brim turned down, the same color. Completely inoffensive, and indeed, no less disguised and out of place than he himself felt, Bellagamba bore a certain resemblance to Mussolini in his last years, it occurred to him, when the Germans had rescued him in an airplane from the ski lodge at Gran Sasso. . . .

"Hello," he said.

"Is this yours?" Bellagamba said, nodding toward the car and barely glancing at him.

He nodded.

He moved beside Bellagamba, and looked straight ahead. It was eight by now. The square was becoming populated. And as Bellagamba talked to him about the Aprilia, praising it as a "good model," and, so it seemed, offering to buy it (for some time he had been looking for a car like this, he said, tough and not expensive, preferably one that hadn't been through too many hands, better if only one owner in fact, which he could then transform into a little truck, because of his restaurant's increasing demands), he couldn't take his eyes off the people gathering in groups that became more numerous every moment, opposite him, over there, outside the low red brick building of the Labor Council, and in front of each of the facing cafés. Other people, he also noticed, women, girls, especially little girls, were constantly being swallowed by the great, dark central doorway of Santa Maria Ausiliatrice, off to one side, set back, on the left, at the end of a vast paved space, like a private square, on its own. Nobody seemed to have noticed the two of them. They all appeared to be concerned with other matters. What matters? he wondered, reassured and yet, at the same time, strangely discontent, disappointed. From the top of the spire, which rose, slender and pointed, behind the church, so tall that on certain fine days, coming from Ferrara, you began to see it at least fifteen miles away, the deep voice of the big bell summoned incessantly to Mass.

The bell tolled. For a moment or so Bellagamba had stopped talking.

Now it was his turn.

"Very well, I'll think it over," he murmured, his eyes still fixed on the spire. "Perhaps we can talk about it later today."

"Will you be coming to lunch?"

A little earlier, in the entrance of the *Bosco Elìceo*, at the spot, behind the desk, where he had left Bellagamba, a man of about seventy had been seated, with thin, short gray hair, a malarial, wan, earthen face, and wearing a dirty, worn, striped porter's jacket. Not at all surprised at seeing him coming from the upper floors, this man had immediately informed him that "Signor Gino" had gone out not a quarter of an hour ago, but hadn't left word where he was going or when he would be coming back. "Then say good-by to him for me, please," he had said to the old man, leaving. "Thank him, and tell him I may be here for lunch."

Lunch? he thought now. He had in fact mentioned lunch, earlier. But what if, instead, calling off all his plans, he were to go back to the city at once?

He didn't answer, in any event. He looked away from the bell chamber, just below the tall needle of the tower, and examined the sky. No more swollen, swift clouds, galloping low over the roofs of the town, but a gray blanket, compact, uniform. And what if he were to go home?

He turned toward Bellagamba. The man was smiling at him with his usual, undefinable expression: vaguely surly, sly.

"Let's go have a coffee," he heard the man suggest.

Bellagamba was treating him, he reflected, with the same intimate, circumspect patience as Romeo. But he, too, wasn't actually mocking him, or secretly trying to provoke him or put him to the test. On the contrary. Unless he was mistaken, Bellagamba wanted only to reassure him, to prove to him that there was no need to go on suffering because of mere shadows. Suggest to him, as a friend, that he should have no self-consciousness, no worries or fears.

"Where?" he said.

"There. At *Fetman*'s."

With his heavy chin, held up by the turtleneck of the sweater, he pointed to the café on the left-hand side of the square.

"They make much better coffee there than at *Moccia*'s," he went on, again pointing his chin toward the right, at the square's second café. "And besides," he added, and winked, "and besides, at this hour, Signor Avvocato, I can assure you you won't encounter any nasty faces at *Fetman*'s. Take my advice."

From time immemorial, the two cafés in the square, at Codigoro, had been obligatory meeting places, not only for the various political leaders but for all the middlemen of the area, and he had always avoided frequenting them: out of instinct and on principle. At *Fetman*'s, in fact (what a name for a bar! Before the war, he remembered clearly, its name had been quite different . . .), he had never so much as stuck his nose inside, not once. And yet, why not? Even now, in 1947, in the midst of the red offensive, at this early hour and on Sunday as well, the probabilities of coming up against some unpleasant character were about the same, that is to say, few. And also: if, once he had drunk the coffee, he really decided to go back to Ferrara (going back to Ferrara at once meant, among other things, also giving up the idea of putting in an appearance, in the late

47

afternoon, at the Cavaglieri home), what place would be more convenient than this for telephoning Ulderico? A greeting, a simple greeting and no more, which would perhaps permit him, in the near future, to take the Codigoro road again on purpose to see him; and the only time he could make the call was right now, before leaving.

"Why not?" he answered finally. "Let's go."

They crossed the square, walking side by side like two old friends: always with that impression, in his mind, that everyone was unaware of them, and, as often happens in fact among old friends, without exchanging a single word.

They waited, then, standing at the counter, to be served. And as they waited (there was almost no one there, in *Fetman*'s: a misty atmosphere, steeped in odors of espresso, grappa, Tuscan cigars: a few customers, anonymous, taciturn, seated at little tables in the rear of the vast rectangular room which resembled not so much a café as a garage; and his cheeks, he could feel, were gradually warming up), his attention was finally focused again on the I.N.A. building. Staring at it, now, through the clouded glass of the bar window, he saw the building as a kind of vague, beige-pink cliff, like something looming and inaccessible. It was really an imposing construction, he told himself, as imposing as it was out of proportion. And this explained why the street, there, with the building at its corner, its ten floors looming over it, seemed so narrow, wretched, dark. His eyes searched the ground floor. There was no visible entrance. In the semidarkness that still persisted under the outside arcades, one after another, in line, were the three windows of the new farm machinery store, which he had noticed fleetingly a moment before, crossing the square. But where, he wondered, did you enter, to go up to the apartments above? From behind, perhaps? He mustn't forget to ask him, Ulderico, in a moment. . . .

In the meantime, Bellagamba had resumed his talking.

He was giving advice. Confidential but respectful (he spoke in a rather low voice, also, obviously, because the counterman was nearby), he was now criticizing the idea of going on, all the way to Volano. What was he going out there for? he said. Apart from the uncertain weather, he felt it wasn't likely he would be able to settle down in the blind until about ten, if things went well, not before. And though the hunters out there, this Sunday, must be very few, since only one had set out from his rooms the past night, to be precise a man from Reggio who, for that matter, wasn't even a hunter, but a traveling salesman in razor blades: what would he shoot at, Signor Avvocato, at ten o'clock in the morning? It was no use: turning up at the blind so late, you always risk coming home empty-handed: or maybe, out of anger, reduced to shooting at a gull, because gulls, unfortunately, were never wanting.

"Would you like me to prepare a nice bed for you, instead?" he added, his voice sinking to a whisper. "If you like, you can come to the hotel, and I'll have it made up for you right away."

He turned to look at the man. Bellagamba was winking, as usual: but this time, his face all flushed, as if he were offering him something exceptional, not to say forbidden. In any case Bellagamba was right, he couldn't help admitting, there was no doubt that he was right. As for the bed, though, nothing doing: out of the question. Better, much better, to get back in the car and be off, to Ferrara. In the afternoon, around five thirty, when he had got out of bed, his own bed, the club, the usual bridge game, killing time until supper, all these resources would still be left him.

"No, thanks," he answered. "Very kind of you, but I don't think I will. Don't bother."

He took his handkerchief from his pocket and wiped his lips.

"If you'll excuse me, I'd like to make a phone call," he said, raising his face to the counterman.

"To the city?"

"No. Local. Codigoro."

The man—about forty, with a fat face that seemed damp, studded with a grayish, three-day beard—examined him coldly.

"Whom do you want to call?"

"The Cavaglieris."

"Why, of course!" the man exclaimed, suddenly obliging, taking a slug from the counter drawer, and handing it to him. "The booth's over there. Help yourself."

The man indicated a kind of narrow, vertical closet of dark wood and glass, set against the farthest wall of the room, beyond the chairs and the little tables. And, as he headed for this telephone booth, he wondered enviously why his cousin's name had sufficed to inspire such politeness. But he was wrong to be surprised by it, he told himself at once. What the hell. Fifteen years' residence in a town of a few thousand inhabitants, with a local wife, a heap of children, and the rest of it: anyone, under these circumstances, ends by becoming as-

similated into his surroundings. Even the least predis-
posed. So imagine Ulderico, with his character, more
unique than rare, which enabled him to seem so confi-
dent at every turn of events in life, always so calm and
cordial! The *Caffè Fetman* was probably his place: the
one he came to habitually, only a few steps from his
house.

He reached the booth and was about to step inside
it.

"Do you have the number?" the man shouted from
the counter.

He turned. Bellagamba, back there, was busy light-
ing a cigarette, his face hidden by his cupped hand;
several customers, sitting around, had looked up, and
were staring at him.

Of course: the number. No doubt it had only two figures. But what was it?

He shook his head.

"No."

"Dial twelve. One, two."

He shut himself inside, and dialed the number. In
the receiver, the bell repeated its ring for a long time. It
had quite a different sound, he realized only now, from
the discreet, muffled tone of the Ferrara telephone.
Rough, harshly metallic, insistent: his ear could hardly
tolerate it.

"Who's speaking?" a rude voice finally blurted: so
rude that he held the receiver still farther from his ear.

"Limentani," he answered, not without some effort,
overcoming with difficulty that kind of amazement,
mingled with embarrassment and repugnance, which
the sound of his own name again aroused in him.

"Who did you say?"

"Limentani," he repeated.

He was talking, no doubt, to the maid: an old woman without many teeth in her mouth, perhaps a bit hard of hearing. Limentani, Edgardo Limentani; he was obliged to repeat it various times, even to spell it. No use. The old woman still couldn't understand. Until, in the end, she answered that Signor Cavaglieri was still in bed, and the Signora Cesarina had just gone into the bath.

He hesitated.

"I'm sorry, I don't want to disturb her," he said then. "But, all the same, would you tell the Signora that her cousin, the cousin from Ferrara, is on the phone?"

"Wait a minute."

Her cousin from Ferrara: this, too, had cost him an effort, to drag the words out of his gullet. And yet, one thing was sure: when she came to the telephone, Ulderico's wife, then he would really be hard put to keep some kind of conversation going. What sort was she, this Cesarina? To tell the truth, he could hardly remember her. He had seen her, in all, a couple of times as a girl, without retaining, as far as her physical appearance went, any special impression, and without having ever exchanged two words with her. Tall, yes, blonde; or perhaps redhead. However, after some twenty years—twenty years!—and with a marriage of that sort involved, and all the rest . . . But, by the way: how should he behave, in talking with her? Should he call her *tu*? Or *Lei*?

Meanwhile nobody came to the phone: and this, despite the fact that the apartment—as the noises proved —was already full of activity.

The apartment. It must be big—he could almost picture it—very big, with some rooms as vast as drawing rooms. In the one where the telephone was, for example, some children were playing with a rubber ball at the moment. There were at least three: and boys. And from the thuds that their leaps, their chasing, their falls produced constantly on the parquet floor, it wasn't hard to form a fairly precise idea of the room and of its dimensions. Far away, very far, a baby was crying: an infant a few months old. But now, closer, there was another voice—of a girl about fifteen, this time—shouting "Clementina!" and since Clementina, shut up God knows where, perhaps in her room or in the bathroom, was late in answering, the first voice begged her to hurry to Tonino or Tanino. "Come out," she said, impatiently, but also laughing: "Come on out, there's no gas. . . ."

He held his breath, he didn't make the slightest movement. He felt that he too was in the Cavaglieri house, hidden behind some door, eavesdropping, spying.

"Goal!" a boy shouted, very near.

"Doesn't count!" another one, smaller, protested. "I saw you, I did, you used your hand!"

"No, it's a goal!" the first insisted.

What a racket, he said to himself, what chaos. He would keep out of it, all right.

And yet, though his lips curved instinctively in a grimace of disapproval and intolerance (you see what happens, he thought, when you burden yourself with children: no matter how big and comfortable, no house has enough space then, life isn't life any more, an inferno), still he couldn't help but stay there, the receiver glued to his ear, tensely listening to the voices and sounds with a kind of anxious, torn greediness.

"Who is it?" a voice suddenly asked, over the wire, the slightly hoarse voice of a little boy.

He didn't like small children, as a rule: they embarrassed him, intimidated him. Even with Rory (it had happened to him early that morning, when he had gone into her room for a moment), his throat often choked up, he almost felt he was suffocating. On the phone, however, it was different, or so it seemed. He could always find something to say.

"Edgardo," he answered. "And what's your name?"

"Andrea."

He heard the child panting. It was clear: he had seen the receiver hanging down the wall; and since his older brothers wouldn't stop arguing about the goal or non-goal, at a certain point he had the idea of exploiting the pause in the game to use the telephone. As a rule, he wouldn't be able to reach the receiver unless he climbed on a stool.

"How old are you?" he asked the child.

"Six."

"Do you go to school already?"

"Yes."

"What grade? First?"

"No. Kindergarten."

Rory at seven, he reflected, was already in the third grade.

"We're a bit behind," he tried to joke. "Are you smart at least?"

"So so."

"What do you mean, so so? You have to study hard. Don't you know that?"

The child didn't answer. His silence coincided with the resumption of the interrupted football game. More shouts, therefore, and running, jumps, thuds. And Andrea was still there, at the other end of the line, with his heavy, obstinate breathing, like a little peasant's.

Suddenly, with extreme violence, he felt himself seized by the desire to be, rain or no rain, at any price, in the midst of the valleys: alone.

After all, he could even hang up, he thought, without waiting any longer for the maid who, he was willing to bet, hadn't been able to report anything precisely, his name or anything else (God knows what she was saying still, to her mistress, through the bathroom door!), he could, after all, quite easily hang up and slip away. The moment Ulderico woke, for that matter, he would understand at once who had telephoned. . . .

And after all: wasn't that, in the end, the only thing that mattered?

Slowly he hung up the receiver.

PART TWO

I

To leave the booth and to imagine that in the valley he would find everything he needed, peace, physical and mental health, joy in life, were a sole thought. He had to hurry. He headed toward Bellagamba, who, seeing him approach, threw away the cigarette: he paid for the slug; and finally, with the old Fascist at his heels, he went off, determined.

"Good-by," he said, as they were outside, on the sidewalk in front of the door.

"This morning they're going to bring me a fine turbot from Gorino," the other man said. "Shall I save it for you?"

"Yes, save it," he agreed promptly, to be rid of him.

He held out his hand.

"And thanks," he added. "Thanks for everything."

He waited while Bellagamba clasped his hand in both his own, thick and hairy, after which he turned his back and began to cross the square.

He walked hurriedly, lifting his face every now and then to sniff the air. No rain, not even a drop. As for the air, ah: now he could smell it, impregnated with that typical lagoon odor, salty and yet sweetish, which clung tenaciously to your clothes, and which, after a while, always had the effect of giving him an appetite. Fine, he said to himself, in a good humor. During that last quarter of an hour the wind had not only started blowing again, but had also shifted. It came from the opposite direction, now, from the sea. If it just held for a while, the sky would be swept completely clear.

In order to pick up the Pomposa road again, he had to drive once more past the *Caffè Fetman*.

Bellagamba was still there, he saw, standing on the sidewalk. He seemed so absorbed in talking with an old peasant wrapped in a black cape (the stranger, chewing a cigar stub beneath the lowered brim of his hat, listened and remained silent) that when, driving by, he saw him raise his arm in an abbreviated Fascist salute, he barely had time to put two fingers to his cap. "I'll be seeing you," he muttered, snickering. And he drove off.

He turned into the little side street dominated at the beginning by the I.N.A. building; soon he was following the line of the river port, full, as always on Sunday, of the dark outlines of boats huddled side by side along the dock; then, after about a hundred yards, he turned left. Beyond the curve, because of the road's pebbles, he was forced to slow down and drive at a reduced speed. But there, once he was beyond the crossing with the ring road, he hoped that the roadbed would be good and firm again. And so it was. He watched the bluish edge of the asphalt approach, and he savored in anticipation the moment, now near, when he could press the accelerator once more.

He passed the crossing; he passed the little road just after it, which led from the graveyard, crowded, especially at the entrance, near the pink outer wall, by the usual groups of Sunday visitors; he pretended not to see the gesture with which a beautiful blonde girl, standing at the corner, all dressed in black and with a veil on her head, asked for a lift; he slipped into third, then into fourth. And soon, never dropping below fifty-five, he came in sight of the Abbey of Pomposa.

How long it had been since he had visited this neighborhood! he couldn't help sighing, as the Aprilia sped swiftly along the final, straight stretch. But he was content, all the same: content that the Abbey, apart from the vegetation which grew much more thickly around it now (a sign, in this case, that the pumps of the Reclamation Bureau had been able to go on working even during these past few years), had survived the war, retaining its old appearance intact, looking like a kind of huge agricultural settlement, like La Montina. Ah, yes, he said to himself, staring at the red, ancient stones of the monastery: with that bell tower to one side, as capacious as a granary's silo; with that church, in the middle, which didn't suggest a church so much as a hayloft; with those tall, plain buildings on the right, placed like farmhouses around the barnyard: in fact, though it was on a larger scale, Pomposa resembled in every respect La Montina. And he was, meanwhile, content also for this reason: that remembering La Montina, repeating its name mentally, for once his heart wasn't clutched in the familiar vise of anxiety, bitterness, fear.

When he was just below Pomposa, he turned right, along the Via Romea, then, after a few hundred yards, to the left, on a road that curved this way and that, plunging, obliquely, into the valleys. He drew a deep breath. To the south, as far as the eye could see, he observed the vast, almost marine expanse of the Valle Nuova; to the north, the bleak reclaimed lands, bordered at the back by the uninterrupted, black line of the

Mesola woods. He felt so calm, by now, so full of energy and confidence (it was cold, and he had turned on the heater: and yet it seemed to him, nevertheless, that the air of the lagoons penetrated the closed car, opening his lungs), he felt so well, in other words, that, a moment later, perceiving in his mouth a sudden acid taste, he wasn't too much annoyed by it. He shook his head and smiled. Naturally. With only the two coffees he had gulped down from the time he woke—and he had been stupid, first, not to have Imelde give him at least a piece of bread, and then, fifteen minutes ago, at Codigoro, to forget to pick up a package of biscuits or some cakes—after all, it was only natural that he should be in this condition now. Before settling down in the blind, in any case, he would obviously have to eat something. Were there taverns, at Volano? Some must exist there nowadays, for God's sake. At worst, anyway, he would be able to pick up, knocking at one of the doors of the village, half a loaf of homemade white bread, or else a slice of plain cake, the peasant kind, with coarse sugar sprinkled on it. In Volano nobody would recognize him. And if he paid, besides . . .

He passed the isolated eel-fishing installation at Caneviè, where in the old days they also used to serve food, but which now seemed completely abandoned, out of operation totally; he passed Porticino, a name to which, as always, nothing corresponded, not even the slightest sign of human habitation. And there, at last, after yet another double curve, Volano, with its low hovels lined along both sides of the road that ran from one end of the village to the other, and with the massive parallelopiped of the Tuffanelli lodge, at the far end, at which, it seemed, the road petered out. He had only to cover a few hundred yards, he thought, accelerating, and then he would know if Ulderico's man had stayed there, waiting for him. It was unlikely. But first he would have a look: and afterwards, he could decide what was to be done.

Rapidly he drove through the half-deserted town, he crossed very slowly, as a sign advised, the bridge suspended over the Volano Po, and stopped next to the Tuffanelli lodge, on the side, sheltered from the wind, toward Valle Nuova, then he got out of the car at once. Not a sign of Ulderico's man. He looked at his watch: quarter past nine. He wondered how long the man must have waited, poor thing. But now what?

He picked up his ears. Silence. Only distant cries of invisible birds, high in the sky. Equally invisible, perhaps on a chain, a dog whimpered, not far off.

He looked around, over the immense landscape that encircled him.

He saw, there, at the edge of the flat territory of water and sandbars, along which he had come, and which the sun illuminated in patches, the towers of Pomposa and Codigoro: the first—closer—dark, bare, thick, heavy; the second, slender, bright, very far away: of an almost metallic sheen, a needle. To the right, toward the main body of the Po and its mouth, the dark compact mass of the Mesola woods; to the left, the empty expanses of the Valle Nuova and of the other valleys farther on; finally Volano, in front of him, after the bridge, the two parallel lines of poor houses, some still with roofs of straw and woven cane. . . . He looked: and he heard again Bellagamba's insinuating voice, the words with which, an hour before, he had tried to dissuade him from going on: "Don't bother to go; take my advice."

And yet, he shouldn't give in, no, not resign himself. The idea of going home at once, again, came back to tempt him now, and he was prompt to reject it this time, without any hesitation. To drive back, in the opposite direction, over the road full of curves that he had just driven; to pass beneath Pomposa again; to cross Codigoro, or at least circle around it; and finally, about eleven, to see outlined in the distance, beyond the windshield, the four towers of the Castello Estense: all this would have done nothing but plunge him once more, he hadn't the slightest doubt about it, down into that same grim well of slothful sadness from which, at a certain point, he believed he had definitively emerged. What if he were to go on alone, without anyone to accompany him? As far as the Lungari di Rottagrande he could go on his own, managing somewhow. As for shooting, he wouldn't be able to shoot at anything, true. But he could bear that.

He could also stay at Volano: if not for the whole day, at least for a few hours. Who knows? Perhaps Ulderico's man, that Gavino, lived right here in Volano. And if he did live here, if only to give him in person the five hundred lire owed him, he should track the man down. His last name was Menegatti: Menegatti, Felisatti, Borgatti, something of the sort. But apart from that question: some private house or tavern, a place where he could stay with sufficient peace and security, a distant place, even for a little while, it didn't matter how long, almost as far from everyone and everything as a shooting-blind lost in the valleys: where could he find such a place better than at Volano? His stomach, suddenly, began to burn again. Again that acid taste in his mouth. He had to have some nourishment; and immediately.

All at once, his attention was attracted by something. On the opposite bank of the canal, hidden about ten yards to one side, on the right of the bridge and the road, he had noticed a long and narrow wooden shack, all painted green, with a roof of corrugated metal. It looked brand-new: as he could see from the paint on the walls, shiny, like mirrors, and the metal roof, evidently fresh from the shop. What was it? He tried in vain to read a little sign over the front door. From a thin concrete pipe, held erect, at the peak of the roof, by four convergent steel wires, thick swirls of black smoke poured out. As soon as they emerged, the wind scattered them. Perhaps that was the refuge suited to his needs, he said to himself, carefully examining the smoke, studying its quality—that might very well be the place.

He locked the car door; he set off, against the wind, toward the bridge; he crossed it, holding one of the sturdy hempen ropes that served as railings on both sides; then he went forward, quickening his pace down a slight slope, toward the shack. He had only to read over the door: FOOD AND WINE, and his mouth filled with saliva. He had been lucky: something to eat, at any event, he would find there, without having to wander around too much. . . . A young man, tall, thin, dark, had meanwhile come to the door. And he didn't move away from it. After shutting it behind him, the young man simply watched him approach.

II

From the way the young man dressed, visored cap, military rainproof jacket with sheepskin lining, rubber boots up to his groin, but above all, from the interrogatory insistence of his gaze, he realized at once whom he had before him. This was Ulderico's man, that Gavino: it couldn't be anyone else.

He waved his arm briskly.

"Good morning!" he shouted.

The young man nodded barely: a brief, slightly stiff bow, rather like a soldier's.

"I was beginning to think you weren't coming," he said then, calmly.

"I'm very late, I know," he answered. He shook his head. "Maybe it's because I haven't come into the valley for at least fifteen years," he added, trying to laugh. "And you know how it is, it's hard to calculate the time. I'm sorry."

"Oh, it's nothing."

He had said "it's nothing." Now he smiled, almost imperceptibly. Did this man consider him capable of not paying him?

It would have been absurd: absurd in any case. He reached for his wallet, determined to produce, on the spot, the five hundred-lire notes which, according to the going rate, he owed the man. But the man quickly stopped him. Please, he said, with a slight gesture of annoyance, there was plenty of time to settle accounts. They'd take care of that "afterwards." For the moment it was better to think about reaching the blind, instead. The wind had shifted, he went on, in his calm, precise Italian, almost without accent, raising his pale blue eyes to examine the sky, and, if they hurried, he might still find some game.

The man was right, he thought—dead right.

"I forgot to bring any food with me," he replied, all the same. "I wouldn't like to go hungry. What do you think"—he nodded toward the shack—"shall I have them fix me a sandwich?"

"As you like," Gavino answered. And he stepped aside, to allow him to go by.

Inside, the shack seemed larger to him than he had imagined.

It consisted of a single room: narrow, deep, in semi-darkness. Along the side walls, at intervals, some slender windows, like slits. On the right, a burning fireplace, with, in front of it, seated and motionless, three old men. Opposite, parallel to the wall, a counter divided into two sections: one for salt and tobacco, the other for food; and behind it, toward the tobacco section, her long raven hair haloed by the faint light from one of the narrow windows, a woman's face, wan, pale, bloodless. Standing just inside the threshold, while Gavino, at his side, showed not the slightest sign of impatience, he sniffed, nostrils flaring, like a cocaine addict, the odor that pervaded the room: the mixed smells of freshly sawed wood and cheap preserved foods. The penumbra; the dry warmth; those three customers, there, glasses in hand, on whose decrepit faces the glow of the flames deepened the wrinkles as if they were carved; the woman's head behind the counter; the odor of sawmill, of salami, of pickles, and so on: he felt as if he had stumbled upon a refuge high in the mountains: exactly the same. How happy he would have been, here, if he could have stayed! he said to himself, now helpless against the dejection he had been obstinately fighting since the first moment he saw Gavino. He had realized at once that he could have been happy, in here!

A little later, emerging again into the air and light gave him a beneficent shock, reanimated him. In the sun, the red tiles of the Tuffanelli lodge glistened, vivid, gay: as if somebody had just finished washing them. Even the water of the Valle Nuova, when, from the bridge, he lingered a moment to look at it, amazed him with the extraordinary intensity of its blue. The water was not only blue far out toward the sea, when the tense, cold wind plumed the surface here and there with foam; but even near the bank, where, in tortuous, half-hidden tongues between shoal and shoal, the water crept to within two or three hundred yards of the houses.

But, a little later still, in the car, along that sort of track, more and more confined by the water, that leads from the Tuffanelli lodge to the Lungari di Rottagrande, he was forced to record new reasons for discontent and bitterness.

The dog, first of all: Gavino's bitch. Young and frisky (she was a cross between pointer and setter, medium-sized, brick-colored), there was no way of keeping her still even for a moment. It was no use his speaking to her in dialect, Gavino, or patting her on her mud-spattered flanks, or pushing her down between his legs, scolding her or even hitting her. Nothing doing. Even when she seemed to give up wriggling, popping up every so often with her seal's head between her master's boots, the car was no less full of her, of her persistence, of her life. There was her smell, but also she wheezed, moaned, squirmed constantly. Why not stop, make her get out, let her run herself ragged, following them, on her own? No use even thinking of that, Gavino had said at one point—in her present state of excitement, likely as not, she would fling herself into the water: and then, when they needed her, there was the risk of not having her within reach.

And then there was Gavino (Aleotti, Gavino, as he himself had stated precisely): or, to be more specific, there were the thoughts that his presence, close by, aroused.

As he drove along, gradually he had learned some things about the young man: he was from Codigoro, he had a wife and a child, from '44 to the Liberation he had been a "fighting partisan" and, apart from the little help he gave hunters, between November and February, hired by the Reclamation Bureau, for the rest of the year he alternated farm labor with jobs as a "construction worker." Not much information, after all: considering that nothing was said about the principal fact, namely if Gavino was still a communist (kindly, patient, a man of few words: from his way of behaving he might yet be one), he hadn't succeeded in clarifying that point.

Still none of this was what upset him, it was, like the dog's physical presence, only more so, the presence of Gavino. Strange, the calmness with which, he felt, this man occupied the space at his side, instead of pleasing him, made him nervous, oppressed him. Every now and then he looked at Gavino's right hand, resting on the greenish rubber boot, just above the knee. It was a large, long hand, a worker's more than a sportsman's: a dark hand, muscular and, at the same time, delicate, its nails only slightly cracked, and it was covered with clumps of reddish hairs; and every time, as he looked at it, he recalled, with mounting embarrassment and annoyance, Ulderico. Could Gavino be a natural child of Ulderico's? From before his marriage? he suddenly wondered, complementing the comparison of their hands with that of their stature, the pale eyes, the small head, the calm, especially, that confidence both men expressed even in the slightest gesture. Well, why not? To wait for hours, practically without moving, and then not to say anything! His devotion to duty, frankly a bit exaggerated, could also be explained in this way.

He turned to look at that hand, to glance fleetingly at the thin, tanned face, its sharp, defined profile. The wind had shifted, et cetera, he said to himself, but still this fellow, like Bellagamba, must consider him at the very least an eccentric, to think of being able to shoot anything this late in the day. Of course: unlike Bellagamba, Aleotti Gavino said almost nothing, didn't permit himself the slightest insinuation; and this represented a considerable gain, he had to admit that. But the vaguely contemptuous expression that played over Gavino's bony cheeks: wasn't it, perhaps, far more eloquent, and depressing, than any words? And as he was thinking all this, he reproached himself for having been the one to insist the man come along in the car. What a mistake that had been! If he had let him follow on his motorbike (before consenting to get into the car, he had gone to entrust it, reluctantly, to the watchman at the Tuffanelli lodge), at a certain point he could have sent him away, rid himself of his presence. Now, instead, they were bound together: inevitably.

For a while now the road, reduced to a mere path, had been running along a very narrow strip of land, stretching straight ahead as far as the eye could see, and flanked on both sides by the open expanse of the lagoons. Now, we should be there, he said to himself, recognizing the places perfectly; and at once, on the right, he saw the poop of the punt emerging between two clumps of tamarisk bushes.

He slowed down, pulled the car off to the left, placing it so that other cars, if any came, would be able to go by; he turned off the engine, pulled the handbrake toward himself; he shifted into reverse, then finally opened the door and stepped out into the air. And since Gavino, busy with the dog, delayed in following him, he went off, alone, toward the boat.

He reached it, touched it with his foot. Painted dark, slim as a gondola but with a flat bottom, it was exactly like the prewar ones. Even the floating decoys—tin molds, wooden ducks, and so on—piled there, to the side of the half-submerged prow, seemed more or less the usual kind: varicolored, as in the past, as always. . . .

He raised his head.

The wind was whistling among the dripping willows and tamarisks along the bank, bending the slender, gray, plumed reeds which covered some shoals opposite. It was cold: much colder than at Volano. But when he had put on his rubber boots, and when, after that, under the duffel-like coat which, in addition to the rainproof camouflaged jacket, he had already taken care to put in the trunk the preceding afternoon, if he put on a second sweater, then he would be all set: he would have nothing more to fear from the temperature.

He thought he heard shooting at a very great distance. He bent forward. Yes, those were shots. Hunting guns. The shots followed one another fairly closely. And regularly, above all regular and continuous.

"You hear how they're shooting?" he said, turning toward Gavino, who in the meanwhile had also got out of the car.

The young man merely nodded. He had freed the dog, who, after moving off about fifty yards, was still, motionless, at the edge of the bank, tensely staring at God knows what ahead of her, out on the water. The two guns, and the package of sandwiches and the soft drink, he had set on the ground, a few steps farther on.

"We'll have to bring the other things from the trunk," he added. "Take the key."

And he turned again toward the valley, trying to calculate where, exactly, that sound of shooting came from. He forced his hearing to the limit, sharpened his eyes. Could they possibly be firing toward the Via Romea? So far inland?

III

He had already taken his place in the hogshead.

He sat, all huddled down, on the uncomfortable little stool on the bottom, and meanwhile he followed, at about thirty yards in front of him, Gavino's movements. The Browning and the Krupp, propped there, opposite, within easy reach; all the objects in the immediate vicinity hidden by the upper rim of the hogshead (all except the punt, which was, instead, almost totally visible); and in the center of the space framed between the vertical, parallel barrels of the two guns, Gavino, out there, the water up to his thighs, bent over his multicolored puppets of swamp birds like a puppeteer over his little stage. He could see nothing else.

He lowered his eyes, and glanced at the dial of his watch.

It was even later than Bellagamba had foreseen, he chuckled to himself—quarter past ten. But what did it matter, to him, after all, whether it was early or late? Having sunk into the same mood of a few hours ago, as when he had waked, he confined himself now, in addition to looking, to listening to the muted whimpering of the dog, tied to an oarlock of the boat, the isolated cries of some passing birds, the usual rifle shots that every now and then started up again on the other side of the valley, along the Romea. That was enough for him, more than enough.

Slowly he looked around.

Considerably reduced, compared to what it had

seemed in the days when he used to come here with Ulderico (at this rate, in another fifteen years the Rec- lamation Bureau's pumps would have sucked out all the remaining water), the Valle Nuova had changed its ap- pearance. It wasn't easy for him to get his bearings. The sandbar of a few square yards, against which the blind was placed: where was it, for example? In what spe- cific point of the basin?

To the right, toward the Pomposa-Volano road, which, on the top of a little embankment as it was, and therefore clearly discernible, he would have said per- haps half a mile away, judging roughly, there was a long, flat stretch of dry land, covered by thick, dwarfed vegetation, tobacco-colored, like the hide of an old workhorse. On the opposite side, to the left, against the sun, a second bar, the same sort and the same dimen- sions as the one by the blind, and the same distance as the dry land, that is to say maybe a hundred yards, no more; and beyond it, also about half a mile away, the line of the Lungari di Rottagrande road, just emerging from the water, with the tiny, glistening scarab's back of the Aprilia right in the middle. Facing him, finally, at no less distance, the shores, lined with poplars, of the mainland. Very well. The blind, then, was in the central part of the valley, at a point almost equidistant from the shores. . . .

The waiting continued. If he had been seated a bit more comfortably, he reflected, and not like this, as if on the toilet, perhaps he could have managed to doze off. He could think about eating, instead. The sooner he ate, the better: that much time saved.

He hunted, groping, at the bottom, near the two cardboard boxes of ammunition, for the package with the sandwiches and the bottled drink. He set it on his lap. He took off his gloves. After that, having opened one end of the package, he slipped out the sandwich, nothing else. He would take out the bottle later.

He sunk his teeth into the sandwich and tore off a piece of it. But suddenly, he was no longer hungry, absolutely not at all: annoyed not only by this but also because the bread (before, in the darkness of the shack, he hadn't been able to see it) was of the French kind: a kind of bread that now, obviously, was invading even the rural areas. And in addition: was this salami that the woman in the shack had put into the bread? It was greasy, all right, ugh, no doubt about that. But tough; and with a rancid aftertaste that reminded him of '42, '43, ration cards, the times when, laboriously, though willingly, he had tried to act the husband, the good husband: the worst years of his life, in fact. . . .

He saw Gavino had finished.

"Thank God," he muttered.

He swallowed with effort. And while, still using his knees as a support, he fumbled with the package of wax paper (the first idea that had come to him was to throw away the remains of the sandwich; then, instead, he decided not to), he watched him come back toward the blind, he didn't take his eyes off the other man.

Gavino came forward, setting his long legs wide apart, and stretching his head from time to time, glancing at the sky. And as he approached, it seemed to him, observing Gavino from below, that he was taller than in reality, growing taller all the time. The dog had suddenly stopped yelping. He couldn't see her. But he imagined her sitting, still as a statue: waiting for her master's decision.

Now Gavino was standing above him.

"A lot are flying over," he said. "Did you see?"

The man's joking, he thought; his expression was serious, but it seemed to cost him some effort to keep a straight face.

"No, I haven't seen anything," he answered. "I began to eat."

Gavino nodded toward the Browning.

"There's some wind, and they're flying high. But with that, you'll manage to knock down all you want."

He noticed the package.

"Was it all right?" he asked.

"Not really."

Perhaps it was because he still wasn't hungry enough, he added, but the salami wasn't the best he'd ever tasted. And besides, he didn't like French bread, never had.

Gavino smiled, or at least it seemed to him he smiled, and then he handed the man the package.

"Would you like it?" he said. "Don't stand on ceremony with me."

He was surprised when Gavino accepted without having to be coaxed. He didn't say thank you, on the other hand. After stuffing the package in a pocket of his jacket, he bent to set the now-empty decoy basket in the boat, and, probably, to pat the dog. Was he insulted? After all, he had offered him leftovers. And bad ones, in the bargain.

"Mind you, I've already taken a bite," he said.

"Oh, don't worry about that."

But he didn't believe this reaction, and he wanted to remedy the situation.

"Why don't you take a gun too?" he suggested.

"A gun?" Gavino exclaimed. He had risen slowly to his full height and stared at him again. "What for?"

The same thing was happening again, as at Volano, by the Tuffanelli lodge, when he, without foreseeing that he would immediately regret it, had so insisted on Gavino's leaving the bike behind and getting into the car. Why didn't he want to take a gun? he said, from the sandbar next to them—and, with that, he pointed to it, extending his arm: he could shoot at all the birds that he, on his part, missed; and after staying away from the valleys for fifteen years, he was sure to miss plenty! But Gavino said no, not for him; he seemed inflexible. Mind you, he added, smiling and shaking his head, it wasn't that the idea of shooting didn't appeal to him. On the contrary. But each man to his own trade. His trade was simply this, now, accompanying gentlemen to the place (he said "now" and "gentlemen," motioning at the same time, with his chin, toward the Romea), and then, when the hunting was over, going around with the boat to collect the dead and the wounded.

In the end, however, he consented.

"All right then," he said, "whatever you say."

IV

He gripped the Browning by the strap, pulled it up, and began to handle it.

He treated it with the dexterity and the nonchalance of a man experienced with weapons, but, at the same time, with a kind of distrust, a veiled contempt. What was he thinking about? Probably about what it might cost. No more than that.

"A fine gun," he said finally, twisting his lips in a grimace. "You bought it in Ferrara, I imagine."

"No. Bologna."

"Ah."

For a few moments he became absorbed in examining the various parts: the barrel, the chamber, the trigger, and especially the trigger guard, underneath, of a different quality of steel: white, opaque, like silver.

"It's new. Have you already tried it out?"

"I bought it last September, and I still have to fire the first shot."

"What's that other one? A Krupp?"

"Yes," he answered. "An old 'Three Rings' from before the war. Made around '28, or '30."

"You could give me that one."

"No, no," he answered hastily. "You begin with the Browning, for now; and afterwards, if you want, we can trade."

He bent over to rummage at the bottom of the hogshead. He found the leather case containing the gauge-reducing tube, and a box of cartridges.

"Here," he added, and handed him both.

The cartridges seemed to interest him more than the tube.

"G.P.," he read, in a low voice, on the box.

He seemed puzzled, all the same, concerned. Slinging the gun over his shoulder with his usual coolness, he flipped off the top of the box, took out a pair of cartridges, shoving them, after having weighed them absently in the palm of his hand, into his trouser pocket. Finally, as he bent over to set the half-open box in the boat, he frowned slightly.

Why? What was wrong now?

"They say they're even better than Rottweil or M.B.," he said. "Faster."

Gavino didn't answer. He was already standing up again. With his body twisted in a three-quarter turn, he was looking to the right, up above.

He, too, turned to examine the sky, then, in the same direction; and he saw, almost at once, a solitary bird at about three hundred feet, advancing slowly toward them.

"What is it?" he asked.

"It must be a heron," Gavino said.

It was a rather large bird: with two great wings, very big, but out of proportion to the body, which was small, by contrast, delicate. It was flying with obvious effort, faltering. Its long S-shaped neck, hunched between its shoulder blades; the vast brown wings, clothlike in their heaviness, open to draw beneath the belly the maximum volume of air: it seemed unable to cut through the wind, and even, at any moment, about to be overwhelmed, to be swept away like a rag.

What a funny animal! he thought.

He saw it fly slowly over the stretch of lagoon that separated the tongue of land from the blind, and then hover, perpendicularly, over their heads: motionless, practically speaking, and gradually losing altitude. It was drawn to this point by the decoys, surely. But before? This far? What a funny animal! It was natural to wonder what had made it fly so long, against the wind or almost, what it had come hunting for, so far from the shore, in the midst of the valley.

"But I don't think they're good to eat," he said.

"You're right," Gavino agreed. "They have a fishy taste, just like gulls. But stuffed, they make a fine ornament."

The heron sank still lower. Now they could clearly see its thin, sticklike legs drawn back, the large, pointed beak, the little reptilian head. Suddenly, nevertheless, as if exhausted by the effort made, or as if, abruptly, it scented some danger, it turned on its back, and, regaining height, in a few seconds it vanished toward the Pomposa spire.

"He must have caught on," Gavino laughed. "He probably said to himself: this isn't such a healthy spot, better clear out."

It was laughable, he realized, but he didn't feel like laughing.

He also nodded toward the shore opposite.

"If only it doesn't go and get itself killed farther on," he grumbled.

"No, no," Gavino answered, with one foot already in the boat. "You'll see: in a little while he may very well come back and take another turn around these parts."

He added nothing further. He pushed the boat into

the water, and then, erect at the poop and dipping the oar, he began to move away.

He watched the man go, shielding his eyes against the sun. He saw him arrive at his destination, climb to the ground, drag up the prow, untie the dog from the oarlock, bend to collect the box of G.P.'s from the bottom of the boat: and finally, climbing to the top of the sandbar, he looked immediately for shelter behind a clump of swamp reeds. Before disappearing almost entirely (he must have found something to sit on: now only a bit of his cap stuck up above the thicket), Gavino had raised his arm, as if to say: "I'm here," and, mechanically, he had replied, with the same gesture.

V

After staring at the long, dense ranks of the decoys, set at intervals in front of the blind, he had dozed off. He had slept, yes. Perhaps he had even dreamed. And now, there, coming from the left, a short, forceful whistle made him start, wakening him.

He looked up.

At about two hundred, two hundred and twenty feet, a half-dozen ducks were crossing the sky over the blind. Ducks, they were ducks all right, he thought, as he slipped the shotgun from between his thighs and propped it against the rim of the hogshead; he could tell by the way they flew, the fast, urgent, palpitating rhythm of their short, stubby wings. What family did they belong to, however? He had never been very good at distinguishing, at first glance, the different varieties of birds of the valley. And ducks came in dozens of varieties.

They flew in formation: one at the head, and the others, behind, in a triangle, like a squadron of little military planes. In haste, like someone hurrying, a bit late, to a specific appointment, they, too, headed toward the Romea. "Bon voyage," he murmured. Unless there were detours at the last moment, they would arrive within range of the hunters lying in wait along the opposite bank, in about a minute.

The birds didn't stop. With the wind carrying them along, it was unthinkable that they would change their course. But he had barely completed this thought when, putting, again, the shotgun between his legs, he glimpsed two of them, two dots which had become almost imperceptible against the dark wall of clouds that gathered, compact, above the mainland, then they moved abruptly away from the group and, after making a broad lateral curve, they began to come back.

He picked up the Krupp again. There were two of them, all right: perhaps a couple, male and female. Passing by, they had spotted the decoys. And now they were turning up again: to have a better look, make sure.

To judge by the slowness with which they grew larger, they must be proceeding with great effort, and it was understandable: the wind, this time, was against them. But, apart from the wind, weren't they also undecided perhaps, hesitant about the path to take? At a certain point—who knows?—they might give it up. Another about-face, and in a few moments they would vanish. . . .

For more than an hour he stayed like that: sitting with the gun in his hand, watching the birds arrive over his head. He didn't shoot. He didn't even try it once. The only one shooting, knocking down, one after the other, the birds that came within his range, was Gavino, from behind his thicket. *Bang-bang. Bang-bang-bang. Bang-bang-bang-bang. Bang-bang-bang-bang-bang.* In series of two, of three, of four, and even of five successive explosions, his shots rarely missed their mark. And the birds, killed or wounded, plunged into the water with dull thuds.

The first to fall had been the two ducks—two mallards, probably—which, after having gone off, until they had almost reached the opposite shore of the valley, had then come back, struggling obstinately against the wind. The same fate, a little later, had befallen a pair of widgeon, also coming from behind, from the sea, which, however, had dropped at once, over the decoys, gliding with opened wings. Then, again, an isolated mallard. Finally, several times, a long line of coots. Rapidly, in other words, the number of birds Gavino shot rose to about thirty. But crouched in the hogshead, he, meanwhile, did nothing. He just sat there watching, and that was all.

It was, always, a bit as if he were dreaming.

The first two ducks, for example, he had seen approaching until they hung, suspended, almost motionless, over the hogshead more than a hundred yards above him. All of a sudden, however, they had dived, headlong, dropping at full speed, their dark beaks open, wide, and their little round eyes also widened, bloodshot; and he had found them on top of him in a flash: suddenly large, enormous. They hadn't attacked him. Grazing his head, they had gone on. But a moment later, *bang-bang,* two shots. And he had felt the kick of the gun in his own stomach.

A coot, too, that had later darted past him, very close, with the hiss of a projectile, this bird, too, he hadn't so much seen, really, as dreamed, he thought. It whistled off, obliquely, at God knows how many miles per hour. And yet he had been able to observe it in every detail: just as if it had been still, photographed, arrested there in mid-air, and forever. The slate-black feathers, lightly tinged, on the back, with an olive-yellow; head, neck, tail, and crupper black; the lower parts just a shade lighter; the wingtips white; the beak, flat, bluish; the legs green, shading into orange in the upper part; the red iris, wide, glassy. As sometimes happens in night-mares, in an instant—the instant before Gavino's five shots, catching the bird on the wing, made it fall into the water like a bundle—he had managed to see every-thing: and to think of everything, in the meanwhile, except of grasping his Krupp and pressing the trigger.

Nothing, any longer, appeared real to him. Gavino, on his sandbar, his forehead wrinkled and the Browning scorching his hands, carefully peering up, around, so as not to be taken by surprise; the dog, crouched at his feet, but ready, after each round of shooting, to spring into the water and bring back to her master, holding them tight and high in her dripping mouth, more birds to add to the pile of dead or dying; he, him-self, seated in the hogshead with the gun in his hand like Gavino, but inert, incapable of a single movement . . . Real and unreal; seen and imagined; near and far: all things became mixed and confused among themselves. Even normal time, the time of minutes and hours, no longer existed, counted for nothing.

Suddenly, and it must have been one o'clock in the afternoon by then, he recognized the heron.

It was flying there before him, two hundred yards off: coming from the north, as it had the first time, and still proceeding with that clumsy, very slow way of moving, like an old Caproni plane. He shook himself. "Stupid!" he exclaimed, silently. The bird really looked like someone who, out of pure curiosity, without the least real need, finally, persisting, gets himself into trouble, on his own.

The bird kept low, he noted—much lower than be-fore. How many feet? A hundred and fifty at most. However little he turned to the left, drawn by the decoys again, he would any minute be overhead again. And with the tube applied to its barrel, the Browning could have brought him down easily.

He turned toward Gavino, whose head rose entirely from the bush. He seemed distracted, he did nothing but move his head. Hadn't he seen it yet? Didn't he deem the bird worthy of a single G.P.? That was also possible.

Still he couldn't believe it. He remembered the words: "Stuffed, they make a fine ornament"; and he regretted not having said at once, to Gavino, very clearly, that he had never been able to bear stuffed birds.

It came forward, now, closer and closer, showing itself to him—and his heart, meanwhile, had begun to beat hard against the bone of his sternum—with extraordinary, almost intolerable evidence. On the little head, perfectly smooth, something fragile stood up, from the back: a kind of wire, an antenna, who knows? And he was just wondering what the devil it might be, that curious thing, and he was narrowing his eyes to try to see better, when, suddenly, in the vast air, sunlit and windy, he heard the familiar double shot resound.

VI

It didn't fall at once. He saw it give a kind of jerk, up in the sky, flap its broad brown wings awkwardly, then veer toward the sandbar from which the shots had been fired. It struggled to keep aloft, to gain altitude. But then it let itself go, abruptly, and came down as if it were being broken into pieces. It really was an old Caproni, he had time to say to himself at the moment when it plunged to the water and sank—the kind of plane they used in the First World War, all canvas, wires, and wood.

He thought it was dead, and that the dog would burst out and collect it. But no: as soon as it surfaced, it pulled itself up on its stilt legs, moving here and there, in jerks, its minuscule head. "Where am I?" it seemed to be wondering. "And what's happened to me?"

It still hadn't realized anything: not a thing. Or so little, in any case, that though one wing, the right, hung limply along its side, it made a movement of its shoulder blades, at one point, as if preparing to take flight. Only then, evidently, it became aware it was wounded. And in fact, from that moment on, it gave up any further efforts of the kind.

Restless, never ceasing to turn the smooth, slightly foolish, *viveur*'s head, prolonged behind the nape by the strange, almost imperceptible, filiform antenna, it still tried to get its bearings, to recognize, if not the places, at least the nature of the objects surrounding it. A few steps away, for example, it noticed the punt, half on land and half in the water. What was that? A boat, or perhaps the body of a great, sleeping animal? Best to keep out of its way, anyhow. Better not risk approaching the little beach of fine, compact sand where that dark, menacing thing lay crosswise: much better. The pain in its side, for that matter, could no longer be felt. If it just avoided moving its wing, it felt no pain. It could wait.

He looked at it, full of anxiety, identifying with it completely. For him, too, the reason of many things was obscure. Why had Gavino fired? And why didn't he stand up now, and fire a second shot, the *coup de grâce*? Wasn't this the rule? And the dog? What was he afraid of, Gavino: that the heron, not having lost enough blood, might use its beak to defend itself? And the heron? What would it do? Wait, yes: but for what, and how long? His head felt befuddled, stunned: crammed with questions that received no answer.

Many minutes went by like this. Until, suddenly, he realized that the heron had moved.

It was heading in his direction, he observed, after he had raised one hand to shield his eyes from the glistening of the water—right toward the hogshead. But it was obvious. The heron had seen the decoys. Colored as they were, and struck by the sun's sidelong rays, they naturally seemed a flock of real birds, busy feeding. It was worth trusting them. There was no danger, surely, around there.

It advanced, dragging its wing in the water, in little, rapid, successive darts, punctuated by brief pauses, carefully choosing the most shallow stretches of water. It passed the decoys closely, came forward, farther forward. And finally he found it face to face, an arm's length from the hogshead, preparing to step ashore. Once again it had stopped. Brown all over, except for the feathers of the neck and breast, a delicate beige tone, and except for the legs, the yellow-brown of flesh-less bone, of relics, it bent its head slightly to one side, observing him: curious, perhaps, but not frightened. And he, without moving, almost without breathing (it was bleeding from a hole halfway along the wing, at the joint), he was able to return, at some length, that gaze. . . .

It had huddled against the hogshead, now, just like a shivering old man, seeking the sun; and he could no longer see it, he sensed it. From time to time it shifted: looking for a better position, or to give itself a shake. Large, bony, disproportionate—and half crippled in the bargain—it judged its movements badly. It kept bumping into the hogshead.

For minutes and minutes, nevertheless, it stayed erect: perfectly immobile. In a careful, sideways position to the cold, whistling gusts of the sea wind, and with the warm planks of the hogshead behind it, what was it doing? It was a bit reassured, perhaps. Though, even now, it hadn't understood much; it still kept looking around. Regain strength: this, for the present, it must be saying to itself, was the chief aim. And once regained, whoosh, it would impetuously spread its wings and fly off.

More time went by: he didn't know how much.

Suddenly three shots in succession, followed by the same number of thuds, shook him painfully.

He turned his head toward Gavino.

"Isn't that enough?" he complained, in a low voice.

He waited until the birds surfaced (coots: all three still, dead), and looked at his watch.

Unfortunately it was only two o'clock; and this light, perfect for shooting, would last another hour and a half at least. And besides, even if he, personally, had had more than enough: could he, at this point, raise his arm and signal Gavino to stop? True, for a little while, the heron hadn't moved at all. If it was still alive, though, what could they do with it? Finish it off with a gun, point-blank? No: that was out. Capture it then? Lean out of the hogshead, pick it up, in his arms, and then take it to the city? How? In the car? And then, where could he keep it? In a cage down in the court-yard? He could imagine Nives, if she saw him come home with a bird like this, and, what's more, wounded, a bird which in veterinarian's fees alone would cost God knows what. He could imagine her shouts, her protests, her whining. . . .

The dog had barely finished coming and going. She had collected the last coot, brought it dutifully to the proper person. And then, turning by chance to the right, toward the strip of land, as if to seek, from that direction, some kind of suggestion, he saw again the heron.

It had already moved about ten yards away from the hogshead, and, from the direction it had taken, it seemed to want to reach that strip of land. The racket of the shooting just now had surely frightened it. Then it had seen the dog go and come three times in a row, returning to shore each time with a coot in her mouth; and, though wounded, though weakened by loss of blood, and consequently more anxious than ever to enjoy there, sheltered from the wind, the last warmth of the sun, at a certain moment it had thought that it was wise still, immediately, to "move on." The long strip of land, over there, thickly covered with vegetation, more or less the same color as its feathers, and mostly tall enough to allow it to walk there without being seen, perhaps represented what best suited the bird's needs. To hide in there, for the present, waiting for night, which was now near; and afterwards, afterwards it would see what could be done. Because the land might not necessarily be entirely surrounded by water. How could it tell? The shoal might be connected, somehow, with the mainland. And having the mainland within walking distance would mean a further opportunity to escape, perhaps even salvation, or perhaps, if not definitive salvation, the almost certain guarantee of staying alive at least until tomorrow.

It went farther and farther away, in the meanwhile, painfully dragging its shattered wing after it; and he thought he could read in its narrow, obstinate little neck all this reasoning. But how mistaken it was, he suddenly said to himself, it fooled itself to such a degree (the strip of land was all right, it would get there; but with all the blood it was still shedding, the dog, soon unleashed to search for it, wouldn't have the slightest difficulty in flushing it), it was wrong to such a degree, obviously, poor stupid animal, that if he hadn't felt that shooting at it would seem, to him, shooting in a sense at himself, he would have fired at once. Then, at least, it would be all over.

PART THREE

I

He wanted to be at Codigoro as soon as possible.

"Good-by," Gavino was saying to him. "If you should happen to need me again, you can always send word by Signor Cavaglieri."

"Yes, of course."

"And thanks."

"Oh, not at all. Thank you."

He had already swung the car around. Through the windshield, he could see before him the hump of the suspended bridge. In a moment he would be off again, at last.

He rolled up the car window, and only at this point, after the rather animated argument that they had had a short time before about the game—he, trying to give it all away, and the other man, obstinate, refusing to accept—he decided to look Gavino in the face. Dignified as always, but almost at attention (his chapped lips, the pale face of a man who is hungry, smiled at him weakly, as if apologizing), and he thought he could recognize this man, suddenly, beyond the dirty pane, for what he really was. A farm laborer making five hundred lire a day, that's what he was. Basically he was just an ordinary peasant, a poor devil.

And yet, a few minutes later, along the winding provincial road to Pomposa, returning to this notion afforded him no comfort. A hired hand, he stubbornly repeated to himself—a wretch, despite his airs, his manner which was a cross between gentleman and C.P.

card-carrier, despite his insistence on accepting no presents, nothing, not even a brace of duck, and not even, obviously, a dead heron, suitable for stuffing by the taxidermist and nothing else, and there was no telling when Gavino, on his little motorbike, with the exhausted dog trotting after him, would reach Codigoro. Still, this reasoning was all useless. Without worrying whether the car, pushed to its top speed, might end in a ditch, or else in the broad canal that, after Pomposa, flanked the road on the right, he took the curves, making the tires scream against the asphalt, exactly as if Gavino, the dog, and everything the two of them reminded him of were following him closely, were even at his heels.

He sped, his hands clutching the wheel, his eyes fixed on the road; and at the same time he was thinking.

At Codigoro he would surely be able to rid himself of the dead birds that filled the trunk: an embarrassing and disgusting cargo which at every curve he thought he could feel, behind him, shifting its weight limply here and there. At Codigoro, too, with the hunger he was suffering (because, yes, since he had left the Tuffanelli lodge and Volano behind him, he had been overcome, too, by such an appetite that he feared nothing could sate it), he would eat, at last: and not only "the nice turbot" Bellagamba had mentioned to him at eight this morning, but everything else he chose to order. And also: the stop at Codigoro, absolutely on the program for that matter, would enable him to delay for at least another three hours his return to Ferrara, which now, mile after mile, was becoming colored for him in hues that were more and more grim and depressing. To dine, in fact, fob the game off on somebody, catch his breath a bit (and Ulderico? Wasn't he to drop in at the Cavaglieri house?), meant that he wouldn't be able to set off again before six. And if, by six, the fog had already come down, so much the better. In that case he would reach home in his own good time: when the table had been cleared, or with all of them, including the Manzoli couple down below, long since in their beds.

A little before Codigoro, passing the cemetery, a black, compact wall of mists, suddenly looming up in front of the hood, forced him to press violently on the brake pedal. It wasn't fog, no, it didn't seem fog. It was probably only a low cloud, which a breath of wind would have been enough to scatter. In the meanwhile, however—at barely three fifteen in the afternoon! —it was as if night had already fallen. That clear air that had surrounded him until a moment ago belonged to a distant past, so remote as to be unbelievable.

He entered the town at low speed: headlights on and windshield-wiper working. He could see almost nothing. The mist, his eagerness to sit down at a laden table, and above all the impression he continued to feel of being pursued, absurd, he knew, but not for that less real, prevented him from taking his eye off the yellowish glow, unswirling, cast directly before him by the headlights. He proceeded with difficulty, as if through a kind of subterranean passage, more and more consumed by his impatience to be in the *Bosco Eliceo*'s dining room. The little entrance hall and the hotel's upper floors he already knew, for one reason or another. But the dining room, obviously adjacent to the entrance, beyond the wall opposite the steps: what could it be like? He imagined it full, even now, at three fifteen, with jolly, noisy people, eaters and drinkers accustomed to eat and drink for hours and hours, in a warm, heated atmosphere, bathed in electric light and steeped in odors, food, damp clothing, oiled leather: and he couldn't help being amazed, since an atmosphere of this sort which, in normal circumstances, he would have faced reluctantly, oppressed, as usual, by the fear of unpleasant encounters, now had for him an intense, irresistible attraction.

Cutting across the dark, shifting lake of vapor that engulfed the square, he slipped into the little street of the *Bosco Elìceo*, and in a few moments he was outside the hotel. Pulled up along the sidewalk to the right, across the street, there were some cars, in a line. There was, nevertheless, still parking space, precisely opposite the horizontal bar of neon, already lighted. As he was parking, he thought of Bellagamba. Perhaps Bellagamba would agree to take the dead birds. In this case, the Aprilia parked right there was just what was required. To unload the game from the trunk, and carry it inside (the light of the neon would make the operation even easier), became then a trifling task.

He got out of the car; since the guns, too, were in the trunk, he didn't bother to lock the door; he moved to the other side of the street, pushed open the glass door of the hotel; finally he went inside, taking off his cap, into the warmth and the odor.

There was nobody in the little reception room: not even the old man with the cropped salt-and-pepper hair who had exchanged a word or two with him this morning. But the confused sound of voices and crockery that came, in fact, from the right, through a double swinging door, immediately made his heart beat faster. So he hadn't been wrong! In a moment, when he was in there, in the dining room, there was no doubt that he would find immediately, if not the dish, all ready, on which he could fling himself, at least the rest of what he was seeking: calm, safety, stability of mood, an exact and balanced sense of things. But then: in waiting for a bit of something substantial to chew on, couldn't he begin with half a loaf of bread and a glass of the *Bosco*'s wine? Drinking had never been a special passion of his, true. Today, however, perhaps because of the damp cold he had suffered in the blind, he felt a great desire to drink. Almost more than to eat.

As soon as he had stepped across the threshold of the dining room, which was a vast, crowded hall, smoky and noisy just as he had imagined it, but half in darkness, however, and with something sad, squalid about it, Bellagamba quickly rushed toward him with open arms. When he first came in, the proprietor was standing, gesticulating, at a table with a dozen or so customers: a distant table, the most distant, beneath a window in the rear wall. He was laughing and making the others laugh: God only knows what story he was telling. But he looked around, saw the newcomer, and immediately dropped the others.

"Why, I thought you had gone on back to the city," he said, raising his voice over the noise.

He clasped his new guest's hands in both of his own. He winked.

"Did it go well?"

He seemed to shelter him with his eyes, all filled with eager concern. Coatless, he was still wearing that iron-gray jersey, with its turtleneck like a cyclist's, the hem hanging down to the crotch of his trousers.

"Have you eaten already?"

He shook his head.

"No."

"I bet you're good and hungry by now."

"Rather. I'd like to eat."

He expressed himself brusquely: much more so than he would have wished. But all this fuss was exasperating him.

"It's all ready, all ready," the other man stammered, intimidated, drawing aside.

He looked around.

"Would you like to sit over there?" he suggested finally, pointing to a little corner table, to the left of the door.

From this distance, he noticed the cloth scattered with crumbs and broken toothpicks, stained with wine, and again he felt an inner spurt of repulsion. Still there was no other choice.

"Thank you," he said.

He went over, reached the table, sat down. He drew a long breath.

"What can you give me?"

"Whatever you like," Bellagamba answered.

He stood facing him, at the other side of the table. Bending forward slightly, he clasped the back of a chair with his hands. Behind him the waiters—four or five country lads, with the dirty white jackets of hospital orderlies—busy as they were, red-faced, their necks dripping sweat, laden with plates, going back and forth constantly between the room and the kitchen, passed by without looking at them.

"I still have that nice turbot," he added, winking again. "I set it aside especially for you."

"Good. Will it take long to cook it?"

"That depends. It depends whether you want it boiled, or grilled. Boiled, it would take about twenty minutes."

He would have to be patient. He lowered his eyelids.

"And grilled?"

"Longer. Thirty, at least."

He opened his eyes again, and he looked at his watch. Half past three.

"Boiled then," he said. "But, in the meanwhile, haven't you something already prepared? Something I can eat right away?"

Bellagamba had bared his closely set little teeth, like an old boxer's, in a nervous smile. The veins on his forehead had swollen strangely. What had come over him? From the depth of their sockets, his little blue eyes were staring, bewildered, or so it seemed. With the anxiety, for some reason, of an animal that scents danger.

"Would you like some fish antipasto?" he had begun to whisper in the meanwhile. "Shrimp, baby squid, crayfish, some marinated eel: there's a bit of everything."

He felt a jet of saliva fill his mouth.

He swallowed.

"Bring me that then," he said.

And as the host was already going away, turning toward the door that led to the kitchen, he added: "Don't forget the bread. And some wine."

A moment later, he realized the heat was stifling.

He stood up, took off the heavy jacket and one of the

two pullovers, throwing them carelessly, along with his fur cap, onto the chair opposite him. Nevertheless, when he had sat down again, he became aware it wasn't enough. The skin on his forehead, his cheeks, inflamed by the long exposure to the sun and the wind, had suddenly started burning. The only thing, naturally, he reflected, his elbows leaning on the table, his face locked in his hands—the only thing would be to wash immediately with cold water. And he was about to get up and look for the ground-floor bathroom, when, seeing Bellagamba advancing at a run among the tables, laden, too, with the dishes of antipasto and bread, with a bottle of wine, and also, held fast under his left armpit, a freshly ironed cloth folded over twice, he changed his mind. First he would put something in his stomach. And afterwards, perhaps, he would think of bathing his face.

II

Even before Bellagamba, wishing him good appetite, had turned on his heels, he attacked the dish of antipasto. This was hunger, not just appetite! He felt he had never been so hungry in his whole life.

He filled his mouth with the sweet-sour pulp of the shellfish, and swallowed: draining then long gulps of wine, or stuffing himself with bread. Nevertheless, he soon felt disgusted with the food and with himself. What was the use? he thought. His head bowed, in his corner—in that heat, in that stink, in that greasy and promiscuous semidarkness—it was useless for him to chew, to swallow, suck, spit, gulp. Gradually as his stomach began to swell, the disgust within him also increased.

Things were worse than ever: that, unfortunately, was the situation.

Again there was nothing that did not irk him, wound him. Between one mouthful and the next he had only, for example, to raise his head, look around the room; and each time, unfailingly, whether his glance fell on the long table, the group made up exclusively of hunters, at which, coming in, he had glimpsed Bellagamba (who had now gone back to it, and had promptly resumed his talking, arguing, his confused noise, laughter), or whether his gaze met that of some other customer, any one of them, but especially a woman of about thirty, dark-haired, pale, stout, heavily made-up, who was sitting very primly at a table not far away (a whore, no doubt: he could tell by her mouth, her way of smoking, her fingernails, the dark suit which was too proper, the little gray fur coat carefully arranged, as if on a coat hanger, on the back of the chair beside her, the huge purse set well in sight on the table, next to the ashtray crammed with cigarette butts, and her eyes, above all, black, dull, a bit animallike, tirelessly looking for customers probably to take upstairs—with the connivance of the owner, of course, of Signor Gino!—to some room of the hotel), each time he was seized by a sense of envy very similar to the feeling that had tortured him all morning in the blind, when, despite the gun in his hand, he hadn't been able to find in himself the strength to fire a single shot. How calm and happy the others were, all the others! he repeated to himself, his head bowed over his plate. How clever they were in enjoying life! He, obviously, was of different stuff, incurably different, from that of normal people who, once they have eaten and drunk, think of nothing but digesting. To insist now on eating and drinking, in fact: what use would it be to him? After the antipasto, when he had gulped down the rest, the boiled turbot, the gorgonzola, the orange, the coffee, he would sink entirely, he was sure, into his brooding over his usual troubles: the old, and the new. He felt them there, in ambush, all ready to spring on him, as before, as always: and all of them together.

From where he was, Bellagamba never lost sight of him for an instant; and he was well aware of it. The birds, he thought. Why hadn't he mentioned them at once to Bellagamba, telling him to take them? Perhaps the uneasiness that continued tormenting him stemmed only from this oversight.

He raised his hand and motioned to him. Moving rapidly among the tables, Bellagamba came over promptly.

"Everything all right?" he asked, with a worried look, nodding at the plate.

He swallowed, then wiped his lips with his napkin.

"Fine," he answered.

He didn't know how to begin.

"Listen," he said finally, "the trunk of my car is full of birds. Do you want them?"

He raised his eyes and saw that Bellagamba was smiling. It was clear: the man thought he was making him a proposition, a business deal. Or else—who knows?—perhaps a little barter: some game against the dinner; and a bed, perhaps.

"Mind you, they're a present," he added. "Don't misunderstand me."

In one gulp he drained a glass of wine, then wiped his mouth again.

"Counting duck and coot," he went on, "I think there must be more than forty birds. And with them, too, there should be even . . . even a heron."

"Of all things!" Bellagamba exclaimed. "A heron. How did you happen to shoot that? One of the white ones, I suppose."

"No, a red one."

He said this; and, all of a sudden, in the dusk, when the shooting had ended—as if the large, earthen, amazed face, bent toward him from the other side of the table, had been blown away—he saw the dog: her muzzle upraised, dripping, and the heron in her mouth. Drained completely of blood (in the midst of the tobacco-colored plants of the shoal to the right, the dog had reached it when it was already dead), how much did it weigh? Little more than its feathers: it must weigh almost nothing, in other words. . . .

He blinked.

"What a shame!" Bellagamba was saying, his lips bent in a grimace of disappointment. "The white herons are bigger, more beautiful, and when they're stuffed they look much nicer. . . . But still, the red ones are handsome birds, too, all right. You want me to take care of it, to have it all ready for you the next time you come? Here, in the square . . ."—and, with this, he raised one arm to point it out to him, the square outside there, with its fog, with its shadows— "here, in the square, we have a shop that does these jobs very well: much better than in the city, believe me. Afterwards, if you want, we can go and see. Today's a holiday. But they keep the window lighted, even on Sunday."

He shook his head.

"Oh, no," he said.

He must have assumed an expression full of disgust: of all that disgust he had always felt fill him at the very thought of a taxidermist's shop (God, he could imagine the smells: a mixture of poulterer's, pharmacy, latrine, morgue . . .). On the other hand, there was nothing he could explain. Better to cut it short. And let Bellagamba go ahead and stand there, observing him with that amazement for as long as he liked.

From his pocket he took the keys to the car and handed them across the table.

"Here," he said. "You know my car. I parked it just outside."

Bellagamba stretched out his hand. Halfway through the movement, however, he froze.

"By the way," he said, lowering his voice, and his round cat's eyes sparkled. "Have you thought it over?"

"Thought what over?"

"Why . . . the car!"

He drew out a chair and sat down opposite him.

"Well then," he went on, with a hesitant smile, full of sudden shyness, "how about this little deal, Signor Avvocato?"

He was the one who didn't understand, this time.

But then, suddenly, he remembered their brief conversation that morning, just before they had separated. And while he was listening to everything Bellagamba was telling him, namely that day after day, without a little truck, carrying on with the restaurant and the hotel was becoming more and more difficult (the side-car which he owned—a Harley-Davidson purchased with a pipeful of tobacco in an A.R.A.R. camp, which besides, with its high power, consumed more gas than a Fiat—was hardly up to the job, by now!), while he listened, and ate, and also drank, he was overcome by a mounting sensation of futility. To persuade him to sell the Aprilia, Bellagamba didn't spare himself, illustrating minutely the various uses to which the vehicle would be put. Nowadays, when it came to wild game, he said, you couldn't just sit there and wait for the individual hunter to bring it to you: if he brought some, fine, if not, too bad. But to meet the demands of his clientele, steadily on the increase, he would have to go and fetch the game directly from the "big-type" hunters, like Commendatore Ceresa and his hunting partners, since they could bring down as much as two hundred pounds, two hundred and fifty pounds at a time (there was no other system: you had to have the right kind of truck at your disposal, turn up in the valley, at the "chalet" around one in the afternoon, buy the lot, and off again). The same thing went for fresh fish, just caught: if you weren't able to set out from Codigoro early in the morning, when it's still dark, so you can reach Goro, Gorino, Porto Tolle, Pila, or even go all the way to Chioggia, to be there when the fishing boats come in from the sea, and to be there on four wheels, above all, rather than come back with just a few pounds of fish, there was no use thinking of getting fresh fish any other way. He talked, explained, gesticulated. And his listener, in the meanwhile, his head growing heavier and heavier, could find no reply. He understood Bellagamba, yes, he understood and approved. His car, of course. Instead of selling it to him, it would almost have been better to give it to him. Along with all the birds in its body.

At a certain point he recovered himself. He looked away. The table full of hunters, down there, in the midst of the smoke. As distant as if between him and them stretched the Valle Nuova, in all its expanse. . . .

"Who are those people?" he asked.

"It's Commendatore Ceresa, in fact, and his friends," Bellagamba answered smugly.

They were some gentlemen from Milan, he continued, all of them big in industry, more or less. Last year, too, from the Reclamation Bureau, they had rented, as partners, a stretch of valley between Pomposa and Vaccolino, a stone's throw from the Via Romea. They usually turned up on Saturday evening: in cars. They ate supper here at once, in his hotel, but then they preferred to go and sleep in the magnificent, luxurious "chalet," completely made of wood, that they had had set up in two shakes, so near the water they could spit into it. Today, they were about to head back. They would reach their homes around nine that night: the fogs of the Via Emilia permitting, naturally.

He rubbed his thumb and forefinger against each other.

"Those are people who spend; they spend plenty," he concluded. "Would you like to meet them? When I come back, if you want, I'll introduce them."

When he was alone, he finished eating what was left of the antipasto, then he stood up. His face was burning more than ever. He had to bathe it.

Staggering slightly, he passed by the table of the woman in the suit, and, crossing the room, he locked himself into the bathroom next to the kitchen.

But, narrow as it was, incredibly evil-smelling, and inhabited besides by old flies surviving from the summer, the little room offered scant conveniences. A little semicircular basin of chipped porcelain, a greenish towel, dirty and wet; on the floor the hole of the toilet à la turque, filthy, half stopped-up with newspaper; faint light; no mirror; not even a sliver of soap.

He turned on the running water, in any case, and wetted his face as best he could. He dried it with his handkerchief. And finally, though he didn't have any great need, he turned in the opposite direction to urinate.

He succeeded only after an instant or so. When had he urinated last? he wondered. And at the same moment that he asked himself this question, and answered that, in fact, the last time had been barely an hour earlier, on the Lungari, when, to avoid Gavino's seeing him, he had thought to screen himself by the car door, it wasn't so much the colorless jet of his own urine he was staring at, as, rather, with a curiosity, a surprise, and a bitterness never experienced before, the member from which the jet came. "Ha," he sneered. Gray, wretched, pathetic: with that mark of his circumcision, so familiar and, at the same time, so absurd . . . It was no more than an object, after all, a mere object like so many others.

III

"Here's the key," Bellagamba said. "It's number 24, on the third floor. I'm sorry to make you climb all those steps. But up there you have the bath handy, and so you'll be more comfortable."

They were standing in the entrance, opposite each other as they had been that morning: Bellagamba, seated behind the desk, the lower part of his face, the square chin and the sagging cheeks, in the circle of yellow light from the lamp; he, standing, his arms laden with his things, jacket, pullover, fur cap, gloves. However, they weren't alone. Behind his back he could hear people passing by constantly: the last customers going away. Out of the corner of his eye he could glimpse them straggling across the threshold of the glass door that led to the street, then disappearing, bent, bundled-up shadows, into the darkness and the fog.

Busy answering the mumbled good-bys of the customers who were leaving, Bellagamba seemed to him suddenly distracted, absent. Up till a moment before the host had been concerned only with him, insisting that he must by all means go up to one of the rooms, for a nap. But now . . . It was clear Bellagamba no longer knew how to divide himself. He would have liked to show him upstairs personally, he kept repeating, and if he, Signor Avvocato, would just wait a little, in five minutes at most he would accompany him to the room.

"Don't worry about that," he answered at a certain

point, stirring himself with an effort from the inertia into which he had fallen. "Let it go."

"Are you sure you'll be able to find the room?"

"Of course."

"Number 24, third floor: the corridor to the left, third door on your right."

"Fine."

"And when should we call you?"

As usual, Bellagamba was looking at him as if he had something in the back of his mind but were acting as if it were nothing. He was rather drunk, of course; however, he could still take this in.

"It's four o'clock now," the man went on. "Shall we say six?"

He tried to concentrate. If he waked up at six, when would he be able to leave? And then, when would he reach home? There was no risk that . . . And anyway . . . But his brain was already becoming muddled again. Better let it all go. Better move, drop on a bed at once. And try to sleep.

Without answering, he passed the desk and headed for the steps.

"Have a good rest!" Bellagamba shouted after him. "And be careful not to trip and fall on the steps, for heaven's sake!"

He began to climb up, his right hand gripping the railing. The jacket, the pullover, and the rest, collected on his left arm, and heavy as if they were of lead; his stomach filled with food and with wine (so full and swollen that he had had to undo two or three buttons of his trousers): each step cost him an immense effort. As he went up, he stared at the dusty, weak light bulb that hung, up there, from the ceiling of the first landing, and he said to himself that, no, he would never be able to climb up to the third floor. It seemed impossible to him, an undertaking beyond his strength. The porthole-shaped window, just a bit below the light of the bulb, was completely blind. A black disk, spent and opaque.

He reached the landing, turned right, and faced the second steps, came to the halfway landing, then started climbing again. Finally, with no reserve supply of breath left, with his heart crazed in his rib cage, and with his head spinning more than ever, he found himself facing the door of the bathroom on the third floor. He couldn't have gone another step, even if he had wanted to. So he stood there, motionless, gasping: his eyes were drawn once again by the little, dark, vertical letters of the enameled plate with BATH written on it, but he was inert, drained of all thought. Around him, absolute silence. Even Bellagamba's voice, his heavy bark that every now and then, up the stairwell, rose from below to daze his ears, it, too, was silent by now. The beating of his heart, his temples; the rattle of his own breathing: he could hear nothing else.

As soon as he was in his room, stretched supine on the bed (his gasping in the meanwhile had calmed down), he tried at once to sleep. He should have undressed, of course, or at least removed his shoes. The light, however—that he had remembered to put out. And if he had the patience to lie there for a few minutes like this, his eyes closed, forcing himself to make no movement, and above all to think of nothing, absolutely nothing, there was no doubt about it: after what he had drunk, he would surely fall asleep.

But there was nothing to be done, he couldn't manage to lie still. He rolled on his right flank, then on the left, then, once more, he stretched out on his back: and in a little while, he knew, he would begin again. How strange: a few minutes before, he had been ready to collapse. But he had had only to fling himself onto the bed and he was filled with a kind of faint, constant series of electric shocks. His eyes, too, were almost painful, he felt them so mobile, restless, alive. He felt as if two little animals had taken refuge in their sockets, swollen with blood until they were ready to burst, and yet eager to swallow more: two tiny, greedy monsters, as prepared to spring and to attack as the ephemeral swarms of sparks, the flickering commas of light that converged toward them from all sides.

Not to think was equally impossible. It was as if a ribbon were unwinding on its own, an irresistible, monotonous rolling sequence of images. There was Bellagamba, for example. Against the dark screen of his jerking eyelids, or against the other, no less dark, of the compact shadows in which, if he opened his eyes, his gaze sank, there, there was that leather-colored face, eternally thrust forward, distorted at every moment by unpredictable grimaces, winks, frowns, strange movements of the eyebrows, the nose, the lips, the tongue. But then, immediately after it, there were other faces: the face of Nives, framed by the pillow, his mother's with, below it, halfway down her neck, the ever-present black velvet ribbon, then Gavino's beyond the glass of the Aprilia's window, and even the others, one by one, the Milanese hunters, Commendatore Ceresa and his friends, of whom Bellagamba had talked so much: the industrialists, the big shots, the tycoons with the deluxe chalet not far from the Romea. It was their money, of course, he said to himself again bitterly, feeling once more offended not only by certain incredible, and surely very expensive, details of the group's hunting gear, buckskin jackets, gloves of pigskin or chamois, multi-colored sweaters of Norwegian wool or of cashmere, strange, special boots, but, even more, by the way their gear had cluttered five or six extra chairs, by the way they were seated at the table, and by the way they talked among themselves or addressed Bellagamba, who was standing, respectfully, host and servant, at the proper distance—it was their money, *i bajòcch*, as Bellagamba said, in dialect, winking, which gave them such confidence, such health, and which makes those who possess it above a certain level seem to belong to a different race, stronger, more vital, more handsome, more likable! Money, *bajòcch, danée*: it was clear that with people of that sort, everything, *everything*, Fascism, Nazism, communism, religion, family quarrels or affections, farm problems, bank loans, and what have you, everything, suddenly, became of no importance.

All at once he saw before him the face of the woman in the dark suit whom he had also noticed down in the dining room: her broad, pale face, the face of an ex-peasant girl, perhaps of the neighborhood, her great, dull eyes, unfocused, her great fleshy lips, laden with lipstick. Before they separated, Bellagamba had shouted gaily to him: "Have a nice nap!" But, as he thought about it now, for what reason had Bellagamba been so jolly? He was mocking him slightly, of course, as you do with those who have too great need of you, of your protection, and especially with drunks. Still, couldn't it also be that Bellagamba had been trying, in his way, like a born pimp, to tell him not to worry, not to give it any thought, since the whore who cost a thousand lire—no more!—with whom he had been seen to exchange glances all through the meal, he, Bellagamba, Gino, would be sure to send to him, at once, up to the room? Yes, yes: that was what Bellagamba was promising, now he understood, with all that sniggering, with his winking, with his insistence, continually, his constant saying and not-saying!

He heard some footsteps in the corridor. Groping, behind his head, he looked for the little light switch, and, having found it, he pressed the button. It was certainly the woman, he said to himself, sitting up in the bed, it couldn't be anyone else. After having announced herself in this fashion, with a sound of slippers, in a moment she would knock. Or else, opening the door that necessary minimum, she would slip directly inside.

He set his feet on the floor, and slowly, buttoning his trousers, he went to the door. His heart was pounding wildly again. He was sure he wasn't mistaken. A question of seconds, really, and then . . . then the handle of the door would be lowered, the door would begin slowly to open, cautiously, inexorably, and he, all of a sudden, would find her before him, that kind of animal, face to face. Well? How would he behave, at this point? Ulderico, from the time when, still boys, they went to the brothel together, had always been extraordinarily quick and brisk, with the whores. Nothing vulgar or brutal, naturally. A few words, then down to business, simply. Whereas he, on the contrary (apart from the fact that, after his marriage, that is to say for about eight years now, the idea of going with a whore had never crossed his mind), whereas he, on the contrary, had always been shy, hesitant, respectful, and requiring long hours, each time, this was the point, before getting down to the famous business. . . .

From the end of the little room, the vertical mirror of the straw-colored wardrobe reflected the image of himself, standing, beside the door: a distant image, barely hinted, as if it were about to dissolve. Well then, how was he to behave? he asked himself, confused—give her something and send her away? Why not? Later, true, he would have to deal with Bellagamba, put up with new or less concealed innuendoes from him, and God knows of what sort. However, there was nothing to hesitate about. Let her come inside, keep her there a while, talking, and, at the end, get rid of her, put two or three hundred lire in her hand: he could see no other way out of a situation like this.

IV

When the handle wasn't then lowered, at a certain point he wondered if it wouldn't be best for him to open the door himself. The key, unfortunately, had been left in the lock, outside. Otherwise, he could have locked himself in, stayed there without all this ado.

He opened the door, and, seeing no one, he stepped out into the half-dark corridor. He looked to the right, toward the landing, to the left, toward the end of the passage. No one, absolutely no one. Was it possible? And yet, there could be no doubt: he had heard that noise of slippers, he surely hadn't dreamed it. Had it been a maid, the cleaning woman perhaps? On Sunday afternoon? Why not? When he thought about it, it didn't seem so strange, after all.

In the meanwhile, leaving the door ajar, he moved along the corridor until he reached the landing. He went to the railing, leaned over and looked down at the dark chasm of the stairs. From the ground floor, along with a bit of light, there came a vague sound of pots and pans, of tables being shifted, of footsteps, of distant voices. It was obvious, he told himself, yawning: they were straightening up the dining room, preparing it for the evening.

Back in the room, he locked the door, then, rapidly undressing, he slipped into the bed, under the blankets. He had kept on his woolen underwear. But he had barely drawn the covers over his nose when a long shudder ran through his body. The sheets were cold, damp: especially down below, toward his feet. And yet there was no comparison with before. With nothing tight around his waist now, he felt infinitely better. Even his stomach was much less heavy.

He reached out one hand to turn off the light, he rolled over on his right side, yawned until tears came into his eyes; and almost at once, with the sudden consent of his whole being, he realized that his brain was clouding over, that he was falling asleep, that he was dreaming.

He dreamed he was once again on the stairs of the *Bosco Eliceo* and once again he was climbing, step after step, with the third floor as his goal. What he was going up there to do wasn't clear. He was going up, no more: and without too much effort, indeed with strange, mysterious lightness. He shook his head. A moment before, down below, Bellagamba, winking, had suggested having him carried on a stretcher by a couple of sturdy youths whom he had recruited as waiters in the nearby countryside (he kept such a stretcher in the entrance: exactly like the one, with rough hempen canvas, used by the Sant'Anna Hospital in Ferrara to transport the seriously ill patients from one wing to another): as if he were unable to stand up, or had heart trouble, or worse. And instead, not a bit of it: agile, serene, he went up the steps as if driven from behind by a favorable wind, as if he had wings. It wasn't night, nor was it early morning. Through the porthole over the first stretch of stairs, the sky appeared an intense, sunny blue. It was two or three o'clock of a fine afternoon in late spring: May, June. The hour just after dinner.

The hotel was full of people. Although there wasn't a

living soul along the stairs, outside of each room on the two corridors of the second floor, at each door, you could see, one beside the other, in perfect order and, some of them, illuminated by oblique rays of sunshine, two pairs of shoes: a man's pair and a woman's pair. How many shoes there were, my God! However, it was nothing to be amazed at. Even if one ignored all those lined-up shoes, it was still clear that the restaurant on the ground floor served chiefly to mask what happened up here, on the second floor and on the third. Each room in the hotel, rented by the hour, hid a couple. They came from everywhere, by car, even from Milan. They talked, they chatted, they whispered, locked two by two in the cramped rooms, each with its miserable porcelain basin, brand-new but already chipped, with its iron bidet, with its rickety little furnishings of straw-colored plywood, with its wretched, crooked little rugs, with its weak central light. And you had only to prick up an ear to catch a kind of buzz, a hum, suggesting something between a beehive and a factory, which ran secretly through the whole building, from wall to wall, from floor to floor.

But there, suddenly, behind him, there was the sound of a metallic object, falling with a clank on a step, making him start and suddenly wheel around. On the lower landing the second floor—appearing from God knows where, there was the same dark-suited woman who, from the moment he entered the dining room until he left it, a little while ago, had never ceased looking at him for a single instant. Crouching, in robe and slippers, to pick up the key which had slipped from her hand, she was staring at him with the same insistence, turning her head in a three-quarters twist. She was no longer so heavily painted: in fact, she wore no make-up at all. She was smiling, and she stared at him: much younger, now, apparently, much more girlish. Finally she stood up, with the key in her hand. And without taking her eyes from his, she stuck out her tongue and began to run it over her upper lip.

He could see only the tip of the tongue. But, from that little bit of it, he thought he could guess it was thick and short: bestial in its shape as well as in color, which was a winy, bluish red. Black and glistening, her eyes also looked like the eyes of certain rural animals: cows, for example. She was certainly from the area, now he was sure of it: a peasant perhaps, one of the many that, hired by Bellagamba as scullery maids, in reality were destined chiefly to the upper rooms, to amuse lonely guests who needed company. But what, after all, was she thinking of? he said to himself, resuming his climb, but still looking at her. Did she think that showing him her tongue like this would make an impression on him? If this was what she imagined, she could put the idea right out of her head. Not only did her tongue make no impression on him, but, quite the contrary, seeing her display it like that disgusted him; it was disgusting and nothing else.

Now, he didn't know how or why, he was coming out of the bathroom on the third floor; and she was still there, again, standing and waiting for him outside the door: in pose, this time, her back against the railing of the steps, and her robe gathered around her legs so that it underlined the heaviness of her thighs.

She came toward him, and staring up at him without saying anything (as if she were intimidated by many things, but especially by her own coarseness and her peasant inexperience), she began to touch him. And he, while he allowed her to go on, and sniffed the odor of roast eel that saturated her hair, thought that, yes, she must also work there, at the *Bosco Elìceo*, and not even as a waitress, but actually as a scullery maid. In a little while, from the bottom of the stairs, the rumbling voice of Bellagamba would surely be raised to order her to come down, to go back to her kitchen, to her sink.

"Let it go," he said to her finally. "What do you want?"

Without stopping her touching of him, she shrugged.

"Me? Nothing." She laughed, baring her front teeth, large and widely spaced.

"Can't you see I have no time?" he answered. "Let me go, come, come, I'm already late."

"If you want," she insisted, her voice sinking to a whisper. "If you want, I can come to your room. . . . What's the number of your room?"

From her accent it wasn't clear where she came from. She hadn't said *vengo* for *come.* She had said *venghe.* If she wasn't from around Ferrara, she must be from the Emilia region, there was no doubt about that. But *venghe*? Could she be from southern Italy? Evacuated from Naples, with her poor family, after the bombings in '42, and then, to make a living, ending up here, a whore in a Codigoro hotel?

"I don't have a room. I'm just passing through."

"Then you can come to my room. It's just upstairs, number 24. I'm good, you know," and again she showed him her tongue. "You'll see how good I am, I'll give you a good time."

Having said this, she took him by the hand and, hastily, her slippers clapping against her bare, callused

heels, she began to draw him after her toward the corridor to the right.

Disconcerted, reluctant, he followed her. The hand
that drew him along was thick, hard, and it seemed
greasy: the hand of a woman who works in a kitchen
scouring pans and kettles with pumice. And yet, not unlike the days when, as a youth, he went to the brothel—
and his cousin Ulderico, for this reason, never stopped
teasing him—now too, more than by physical repugnance, he felt blocked by a fear: the fear of venereal
disease. Without a contraceptive, he could easily as not
catch the clap, or even syphilis. And if he had at least
felt some desire, after all, to go and do what they were
going to do! But how would it have been possible, in any
case, at seven forty-five in the morning, and with nothing but a cup of coffee inside him? No, no, a moment
from now, in the room, politely or rudely, he would get
rid of her. Two hundred lire, three hundred: just so she
would earn a little something anyhow. He wouldn't
spend more than that.

And finally they were in the room: she in bed, under
the blankets, he, standing, at the window, from which
he could see, in the dusk streaked by huge galloping
clouds, the same things as from the window of the
bathroom, the chicken run with its hens, the playing
field with the ancient facing goals, et cetera et cetera:
and the countryside, flat and endless, all around the
town, in the background.

It was pointless for her to insist, he was saying, without turning to look at her. He hadn't come to Codigoro
to stop there, but to go on to the valley, to hunt. He had
made an appointment for quarter after six, at Volano,
with a man who would go with him to the Lungari di

Rottagrande. Now, as she could see for herself, it was eight o'clock. From Codigoro to Volano, with the car, would take at least another half-hour; and so, even if he left immediately, he would reach his destination almost three hours late. Could he stay? Obviously, no.

"Don't you want me to try kissing it at least?"

What a bore, what a nuisance! Still he turned, he moved from the window, and unbuttoning himself in front, he approached her until his abdomen was at the level of the bed.

"What do you think you'd kiss? Can't you see the state it's in?"

"You're really in bad shape," she murmured then, without touching him again, and just looking at him, there, where he, too, was looking. "You've got nothing at all."

V

He woke abruptly, not understanding, at first, where he was. But, even before he could reach, with his hand, the light switch behind his head, he regained a minimum of awareness. So he had slept. Slept and dreamed. But what about his call? Why had nobody turned up? It seemed to him that hours and hours had gone by from the moment when he dozed off. Perhaps it was already two or even three o'clock in the morning.

He turned on the light, rolled over on his side to take his watch from the top of the little night table. He glanced at the dial. It was five forty-five. And he immediately realized, feeling at the same time an unexpected pang of anguish, that he had slept only an hour. Tomorrow was still far, very far away. Between him and it there opened the immense abyss of a whole night, one of the longest nights of the year.

After about ten minutes he went down the steps into the gradually stronger odor of stale food.

Below, in the entrance hall, behind the desk, as usual, Bellagamba was trying to make a little radio work. It was broadcasting the sports news: the results of the Sunday football games. He approached. Bent over the radio crackling with static, the old Fascist seemed not to have noticed his presence. He had come down at the most inopportune moment, he fully realized that. On the other hand he really had to leave now. And before leaving, he had to pay his bill: for the meal and for the use of the room.

Nothing doing. No matter how much he insisted, the other man wouldn't hear of it. Apparently, he said, and his voice was louder than the radio—apparently the Signor Avvocato wanted to joke. A fine thing. After all the game he had given him! Please, he wasn't even to mention money. Otherwise he would be forced to give him back the birds, or really work out their value. And then they would see who, of the two of them, was the real debtor.

He turned off the radio.

"But, tell me, did you sleep well?" he inquired.

"Not bad."

"But for such a short while! How long did you sleep? No more than an hour and a half. You said you wanted to be called at six. But I would have let you sleep on, instead. . . ."

He smiled with his sly manner.

"I was already thinking, in fact," he went on, "of calling the city, the Signora. Only so she wouldn't worry, with this fog."

He slapped his hand, closed into a fist, against his forehead.

"That reminds me," he said. "While you were upstairs, there was a phone call for you."

He raised his arm and pointed outside.

"It was a local call, from Signor Cavaglieri's house. And they said that when you woke up, would you do them the favor of calling back."

He winked, and asked: "Isn't he your cousin? The engineer?"

He nodded.

"But who actually called?" he asked in turn, unable

to control his voice properly. "Was it Signor Cavaglieri himself?"

"Oh, no. I don't think it was even the Signora Cavaglieri."

It must have been the maid, he thought, the same old woman as this morning.

He stretched out his hand across the desk.

"Good-by," he said. "I have to be going. And thanks."

"If you like," Bellagamba answered, clasping with obvious reluctance the fingers offered him, "if you like, you can telephone from here."

And, with this, he drew the telephone from under the desk.

"No, thanks all the same," he said, sketching a smile and shaking his head.

He covered the back of Bellagamba's right hand with the palm of his own, then, turning, he walked toward the exit.

As soon as he was in the open air, however, he stopped: uncertain, all of a sudden, whether he should go to the *Caffè Fetman* on foot or whether, instead, he should actually take the car. But he immediately decided on the car. To be sure, he argued, crossing the street, with the gray, coated tongue he had seen a moment before, in the mirror over the basin in the room, a little walk could only do him good. But it was also true, however, that if he went on foot, he would then have to see Bellagamba again afterwards. He could imagine the scene. Himself, coming back from the square, and there, waiting for him, appearing at the right moment behind the steaming panes of the *Bosco Elìceo*'s front door, the face of Bellagamba, distraught, as if thinned, by his usual mania for spying, guessing, knowing. . . .

After he had started the engine, swung around, and was driving dead slow toward the square (the fog, thicker and thicker, didn't allow him even to shift into second), he felt suddenly, totally reanimated. Thank God. If the Cavaglieris hadn't called, it was likely that he, on his own, would never have summoned the strength to telephone them. With nothing to cling to, no excuse to stay a bit longer at Codigoro, there would have been no course left him but to take the road for Ferrara. And at this hour he would already have been on his way, advancing through the fog with his eyes wide, and like this, always, in first gear, for miles and miles.

He imagined, at the same time, the Cavaglieri house: warm, filled with light, with them, husband and wife—already middle-aged, to be sure, and yet somehow still young, still active—and with all six children, boys and girls, from the youngest to the older ones, making a noisy circle around their Papa and Mamma. And he couldn't understand why, now, the prospect of being received there, in the midst of that inevitable racket, instead of repelling him, attracted him, filled him with desire and hope. Who knows? he daydreamed—perhaps, later, after the cup of tea, after the slice of cake kneaded and baked in the house, after the glass of sweet Albana to be sipped slowly along with the cake, they would all insist that he stay to supper, and then, even later, at the end of the supper, and the probable games of tombola that would follow it, that he spend the night there, with the family, like an old bachelor uncle made bitter and taciturn by too much solitude, in a makeshift bed: perhaps in the room of the youngest child, that Tonino, or Tanino, or else in the next-to-youngest's, Andrea's, the one he had talked with for a fairly long time over the phone that morning, and with whom it would therefore have been simple, simpler than with any of the other children, to start chatting in the darkness, waiting until his eyelids decided to become heavy. Perhaps it would end just like that, he said to himself. And it was really something to wish for.

He started obliquely across the square, never losing sight, to guide himself through the fog, of the little dark central cusp, the Monument to the Dead, and, beyond it, barely distinguishable, the façade dotted with little bare windows from which came a white, vivid light, more appropriate to the city than to this town, the enormous I.N.A. building; and he finally came to point the car at the *Caffé Fetman* and stopped. He was now so eager to telephone that, when he had cut off the engine and stepped out, he forgot to lock the door, as he usually did. He remembered it only a moment later, when, having stepped onto the sidewalk, he was about to go through the door of the café. He turned to glance back at the Aprilia. No, he decided, it wasn't necessary: it absolutely wasn't worth it. What with telephoning and the rest, he would manage it all, at most, in a couple of minutes. And in that time, with the deserted square—all of them locked in their homes, the inhabitants of the town, and the others, the foreigners, already gone, already far along the roads to their own homes—nobody would think of stealing anything from him.

He went inside.

The smoke, the steam, the noisy crowd (many customers of the *Bosco Eliceo* had moved here, to argue heatedly in front of the football results, posted on a card on the wall), and especially the sardonic grin with which, seeing him approach, the same filthy forty-year-old of this morning greeted him from behind the counter: all this, in other circumstances, would have aroused in him the familiar sensation of repulsion, composed of his disgust at physical contact, his irritation at noise, his fear of unpleasant encounters. But in the mood he was in at the moment he paid no attention to anything. He asked for a slug; he ordered a Fernet: and deciding to drink it, the Fernet, after he had telephoned, he headed straight for the booth at the back of the huge room.

He turned on the light. Not bothering to shut the door after him, he dialed the number: 12.

Almost immediately, in the receiver, a woman's voice said:

"Yes?"

VI

It was Cesarina, Ulderico's wife: in person.

Calling him *tu*, with the greatest naturalness, not merely as if they had known each other for years, forever, but also as if they had spoken to each other only a few hours earlier, she immediately began to reproach him, affectionately, for having delayed so long before calling. But why, after all, she said, instead of going to eat at Bellagamba's, and even resting there, at his place (luckily, after lunch, they had had the idea of telephoning), why hadn't he thought of coming directly to their house? Rico would have been overjoyed. And as for the children . . .

She had a low, warm, drawling voice, slightly whiny, and her accent was exactly like Nives's. And though the *tu* which she had addressed him with had, at first, somewhat taken him aback, he soon acknowledged that it was best. In a little while, when they met, everything would go smoothly, without too much embarrassment for either of them.

"Just a moment," he said.

He turned to shut the door of the booth.

"It was after three o'clock," he added, "and I didn't want to disturb you."

"Disturb us!" she exclaimed. For heaven's sake: he wasn't even to say such a thing. On Sunday—and now, during the holiday season, it seemed always to be Sunday—they all got up much later, so they were in the habit of never sitting down to dinner before two, or half past. But apart from that: another plate at the table—what difference could it make? If there was food for nine (or rather, for ten, with their daily maid), there was always food also for eleven. And what trouble was it to prepare a bed for a nap after dinner?

"Thank you," he answered. "Next time I won't stand on ceremony."

"Good. That's the way to talk. And how was the hunting?" she went on. "How did it go? Did you shoot anything? This morning, as soon as Rico found out you had been here early, he promptly stuck his head out of the window and said, with this weather, you'd risk not finding a thing. But it was nothing but envy," she added, laughing, "and besides, it seems to me that the weather changed at a certain point."

When he had closed the door of the booth he could hear her even better. She linked one sentence to the next with a kind of greedy little whine: a sound that came half from the throat and half from the nose. And she seemed to him so close, now, that at one moment he even thought he heard the rustle of a sheet. Was she in bed? The promptness with which, a moment before, she had answered the telephone led him to suppose she was. It wasn't so extraordinary, after all, that even in Codigoro there were extension phones and you could attach the phone beside the bed. The phone at the *Bosco Eliceo* must be the extension kind, too.

"Yes, it changed," he confirmed. "We shot, all told, about forty birds."

He was forced to listen to her enthusiastic cries, her congratulations, which were not without, so it seemed to him, a certain air of mockery: as if Gavino, who, for that matter, could easily have telephoned ahead of him,

132

had already given a blow-by-blow account of how, in reality, the hunting had gone. For that matter, he said to himself, feeling once again the secret rasp of anguish grating him, and still not resigned to undergo it, that anguish, to fall into that trap again—for that matter he couldn't have behaved differently. Gavino or not, he didn't like to seem to have come back from the valleys empty-handed. Even if he had to return to Bellagamba's and take back a brace of duck, to carry as a present (and God only knew what it would have cost him, to return there: for an infinity of reasons!), he was absolutely determined not to cut that sort of figure.

But she, in the meanwhile, had already changed the subject. She was asking him about Nives, who, she said, she hadn't seen for at least twenty years: and the fault was mostly her own, she admitted, since, being a real stick-in-the-mud, she had never felt like setting foot in Ferrara; she asked him about his little girl; she asked him how they had spent the war years, the worst of them; and if it was true—so Rico had told her—that at one point they had been forced to flee abroad. And he, answering her questions one by one, began to wonder why she was keeping him on the telephone for such a long time. What about Ulderico? Why did she speak of him indirectly? Why didn't she decide to put her husband on the line? If they were to meet, they should get on with it; and enough of all this chatter.

But, along with these thoughts, he felt other, quite different thoughts, beginning to creep into his mind. He remembered what, only ten minutes earlier, inspired, obviously, by the ideas he had had that morning, speaking on the telephone with the old maidservant and the child, he had imagined he would find in the Cavaglieri

133

home: that is, the whole family gathered together, and the tea, and the cake, and the great oval table for supper, bathed in light, and the tombola game, after supper had been cleared away, or rummy, which they would play just to pass time until the moment came for bed, et cetera et cetera; but something had been telling him, for a little while now, that he had been mistaken, that this was an illusion. How beautiful it would have been really to be the old misanthropic uncle whom the nephews eagerly warmed and consoled with their affection and their gaiety! The trouble is that this, for him, would never have been anything but a part; and a part, moreover, impossible for him to play.

"How's Ulderico?" he asked.

Oh, Rico, he was fine, Cesarina exclaimed, laughing. So were the children, thank God. . . . But Rico, after waiting and waiting, had finally become fed up staying there in the house with nothing to do, and he had gone out (but by eight, at most, he would surely be back); and the children, too—since she had felt like lying down for a while, and they, instead, with their bang-bang, the usual racket, had started playing ball in the living room—they, too, were now out of the house. Toward five, she had sent them to the movies with Giuseppina, the old dry nurse who had brought them all up. They wouldn't reappear before seven thirty.

"But . . . where did he go?"

"Who? Rico?" and again she laughed. "How should I know? Maybe he's gone to see a mistress."

She was joking, of course, he thought. She seemed to be, surely.

"Oh, a fine thing," he said, forcing himself to continue the joke, but with his throat, suddenly, dry. "And where does he have a mistress? Here in Codigoro?"

"No, no, I was only joking," she answered.

Perhaps he had just gone out for a stroll, poor Rico, she added, or perhaps he had ended up somewhere playing billiards, or cards. . . . Five minutes ago, in fact, he had called her from a café to ask if, by any chance, he had called, and to ask, among other things, where the children were. And this meant that, almost certainly, he would then collect them at the exit of the theater, to take them to church with him.

She emitted one of her strange yelps: a little longer and more emphatic than usual.

"But you . . . ," she went on, "where are you calling from?"

"I'm in the square, at *Fetman*'s."

"Just next door then!" she cried. "Have you taken a look around, to see if Rico is there?"

He hadn't had time to notice, really. If Rico had been there, however, the counterman, given his meddlesome nature, would surely not have failed to inform him immediately.

"I don't believe he's here," he answered.

"In that case," Cesarina said impetuously, "why don't you come on up to the house? Do come, and I'll get up and fix you a nice cup of tea."

Even before he could answer, she began to explain where the house was, and how he should go about finding it. They were just a few steps from the square, she said, and at most a hundred yards from the *Caffè Fetman*: and, to be exact, in that big ten-story building on the square at the corner of Via della Resistenza. He should pay attention, though. To reach the inner court-yard and the elevator, he wasn't to come in from the square, the entrance where, for that matter, there weren't any proper doors, but he was to enter by number 7 on Via della Resistenza. Eighth floor, apartments 17 and 18. He could ring the bell from below, and she would open the door for him.

"Thanks," he said. "Very well. I'll be right there."

"Really? Shall I put the water on for the tea then? Mind you, I'll be expecting you."

"See you later then."

He hung up and came out of the booth.

He picked his way through the crowd, looking around carefully. No: tall as he was (over six feet, if he remembered correctly), Ulderico would have been immediately noticeable, if he had been there. He might have gone into some back room, however, to play billiards or cards.

"Have you seen Signor Cavaglieri?" he asked the counterman, as soon as he was facing him.

"No. Not today."

"Thank you," he said.

He turned his back and started toward the door.

"Signor Avvocato!"

He started, then turned around.

From behind the counter, through the smoke, through the steam from the espresso machine, the counterman was staring at him.

"The slug," he said. "The slug and the Fernet."

PART FOUR

PART FOUR

I

When he came outside (funny: there was hardly any fog now), the first thing his eyes fell on was the hood of the Aprilia. As he saw it from the sidewalk, tilted slightly to one side and with the windshield completely clouded over, it seemed to him even older than it really was: a kind of rusted, useless piece of scrap iron. "To hell with it," he grumbled, shrugging one shoulder. His head had begun to swim again. It had been that little glass of Fernet. He should have drunk it more slowly, and not drained it, as he had done, all in one gulp.

He stepped down from the sidewalk and went over to the car.

After locking the right door, he raised his eyes and looked up. Beyond the car's curved roof, the I.N.A. building loomed before him, higher than ever, massive, threatening. A hundred yards away? Perhaps because of the air, now cleansed and limpid, the building seemed to him even nearer. Through many of the little shutterless windows that dotted the angular façade, half on the square and half along the Via della Resistenza, he could clearly see the interiors of the apartments, with people going and coming from room to room, men in shirt sleeves, women, children. Starting from the ground floor, he counted up to eight. There, at the third floor from the roof, no light shone. This meant that the master bedroom overlooked the courtyard. Or else that Cesarina had already left it, and, having turned off the light, had already gone into the kitchen.

He walked around the car and started toward the building.

He was thinking of Cesarina. What sort of girl had she been, this Cesarina, when, in her young days, Ulderico had begun to run after her? He still couldn't recall clearly. From her voice, however, he thought he could tell the kind of woman he would be dealing with in a little while. He had been aware of it from the beginning. He had only had to hear, in the receiver, that "yeeess" of hers, drawled and whining. She must be large, heavy, calm: the very opposite of Nives. One of those handsome women of about forty, in other words, who had always upset him to such a degree that even now, at his age, whenever he encountered one on the street, he preferred to pretend, even to himself, that he hadn't noticed her, that he hadn't seen her at all.

He went over their telephone conversation again: and her words, together with the fact that she was alone in the house, gave him the gradually more precise sensation that he was faced by something decisive, pressing: a kind of crossroads. The more he thought of her behavior, apparently so frank and cordial, the more decidedly ambiguous it seemed to him. That *tu* she had begun with, for example! But the rest, too, namely her introducing him point-blank into the intimacy of their family life (she and Ulderico who lazed on Sunday until late in the big double bed, as the children slept in theirs), and that rustle of sheets especially, which at a certain point she had carefully insinuated into his ear: even the rest, after all, was no less revealing of her true intentions. And finally: what need was there for her to tell him, even as a joke, that Ulderico had gone out to visit a mistress? The truth was that, with those words, she had meant to repeat to him, one more time, so that he would understand clearly, that she was alone in the house, alone, all alone, and that her husband and the children wouldn't show up for a couple of hours. Nothing to fear, therefore: he could come on up. There was time, oh, plenty of time! The apartment, for that matter, had two main doors: number 17 and number 18. And if the necessity were to arise, she could always help him slip out through the service entrance.

Having reached the foot of the building, he stepped onto the sidewalk, and went under the outer arcade along the ground floor. His heart was pounding, he breathed with difficulty. To calm himself, he headed for one of the windows of the agricultural machinery shop, putting his face to the grille-shutter rolled down over it. In the midst of the smaller machines, he recognized, beyond the metal antitheft screen, beyond the thick glass pane of the window, a big American tractor, a Caterpillar. In the faint light of the shop, he could just discern that it was painted yellow. It was an enormous dark mass. Something blind and formless, destitute of any function whatever.

But what a whore she was, he kept saying to himself, what a real whore!

After he had lived together, for years and years, with a woman of that sort, it wasn't surprising that a man like Ulderico, who, as a boy, used to spit on priests as much as on rabbis, had ended up spending his Sundays in church, going to Benediction. One way or another, God knows what she had done to him, a woman like that, he was probably an old man. In record time she had produced six children for him. But now, having drained him well and good, now, obviously, she had turned to cheating on him at full tilt, before the whole town, and it didn't matter with whom: with the counterman of the *Caffè Fetman,* perhaps, counterman and proprietor, or else, why not, with that same Aleotti Gavino, sporadically at her husband's orders, and serviceable, obviously, for all uses. Big, heavy, calm. And whorish, above all. What was the harm in it? she was perhaps thinking at that very moment, waiting for him to arrive. If in the list of her men there was a laborer of the Aleotti Gavino type, young and strong, of course, but still a laborer, why shouldn't the cousin from Ferrara also be added to it? He wasn't so young any longer, the cousin from Ferrara, still he was a gentleman, for sure: just like Rico, if not more so. And then, kinship apart, hadn't they been great friends, he and Rico, as young men, actually inseparable, so much so that until she had become his mistress, Rico's, his kept woman, they had been accustomed to go whoring about together, and often, to trading their women?

Number 7 of Via della Resistenza was a doorway of modest proportions, situated at the very end of the building: at the point where, at the end of the arcade, the town's usual low houses began again. He saw it at once: the moment he had turned the corner. It had been the little vertical plate with the names of the tenants, set under glass, on the right jamb and faintly lighted from inside, which had made him recognize the door from the distance.

Hastening his steps, he walked in that direction. He felt as he had when still a boy, immediately after his exams of the third year of the liceo: the first time that, accompanied by Ulderico, he had stepped over the threshold of a brothel, he couldn't remember exactly whether it was in Bologna or in Padua. Or else, as in the mountains, when he and Ulderico used to drive up there in the August vacations: when, having reached the foot of a Pala or a Tofana, there was nothing left to do but muster up his courage, overcome the nausea that, inevitably, at that moment, gripped his stomach, and, after allowing himself to be roped up, set off behind the others toward a fate from which no power in the world, except the will of those who were drawing him on, could have saved him.

He approached. He bent over to read the name plates. He read: CAVAGLIERI ULDERICO, ENGINEER.

And as, simultaneously, he raised his wrist watch to the reddish light (it was six thirty), and calculated the time which, in fact, he had at his disposal to do what he had to do, and told himself then that, true enough, in the old days, his hunting Sundays, his and Ulderico's, had always ended like this, with a big feed, and then bed with some local woman, a seamstress, a dressmaker, a working girl, peasant: a girl to possess—driving her out to La Montina, himself, if necessary—to pay off somehow and, at the end, to exchange between cousins, between friends, and then to drop automatically: suddenly, seeing the dial of his watch beneath his eyes, the minuscule, calm, round, familiar, gold-framed face of his Vacheron-Constantin, suddenly he was overcome with the harsh certitude that he was raving. He was raving, yes: and had been since God knows when. Since that morning, since the moment when he had waked up, and then, gradually, through the whole day, until now, he had done nothing but rave. He was still raving. Codigoro: those arcades . . . With a sudden lucidity, he surprised himself by wondering: he, he himself, in his hunting clothes, with the fur cap on his head, at that hour, under those arcades, who was he, who, really?

He took off one glove. With his index finger he grazed the bell: not to press that button, but only to touch it, to feel its consistency. He straightened up, finally. And, coming out from the arcade, and keeping close to the walls of the houses, he walked along the left-hand sidewalk, on the opposite side of the square, toward the river port.

II

It was seven o'clock, more or less.

Perhaps the right thing to do would be to take advantage of the fact that there was hardly any fog now, he reflected, and instead of staying there, wandering around Codigoro, staring at the stones of the sidewalks, go back toward the square, telephone again, first, to apologize to poor Cesarina, then get into the car, and be done with it, go straight back into the city. Only, each time a plan of this sort presented itself to his mind, he immediately rejected it. Stay here, then? But to what end? Before its eyes, from loss of blood, had become hooded, the heron must have felt much as he felt now: hemmed in on all sides, without the slightest possibility of escape. With this difference, however, to his disadvantage: that he was alive, quite alive; that he hadn't lost so much as one drop of blood; and that he could have faced the dog, assuming that at some point one might come toward him, only like this: his eyes open, wide.

He walked in haste, now at the end of the Via della Resistenza, determined not to glance toward the great lighters and the barges lined up, as they had been that morning, along the bank of the river port. But once he had sensed at his side the presence of these mouse-colored, immobile forms, so immobile that you would think they were resting, rather than on water, on the mucky bed of the river, he couldn't resist the temptation to stop and look at them.

He had seen boats lined up in that way countless times, especially as a boy, in the canal ports of Cesenatico, Cervia, Porto Corsini: in the days of the blissful, endless holidays that were the custom then, before the first war and immediately after it. But from these—low, broad, and surmounted, not by vast, gay sails of bright colors, but by pitiful skeletal rigging in which, light and transparent as gauze, lazy shreds of fog lingered—from these there was no extracting any sense of joy, of life, of freedom. On the deck of a barge anchored far from the dock, almost in the center of the stretch of water before it, two people were moving: a man and a woman. The man, if he could make him out properly, was old and corpulent, with white hair and the black jersey of a last-ditch Fascist; the woman, a young girl, blonde, wore a homespun tunic and tight slacks, like blue jeans. They were shouting, gesticulating, chasing each other around the cabin of the vessel, from whose window came a weak, weak light, a lantern's. Their shrill cries, remote, like the cawing of birds in the valley; the clack-clack of their clogs on the planks of the deck; their grotesque shadows, enlarged by the yellowish light that came up from the hold . . . Powerless, as he was, to go any closer, he seemed to watch, from the edge of an endless square, a puppet show being put on for him alone. It was useless: the old man, the villain, in the end, would succeed, naturally, in laying his hands on the beautiful maiden he was pursuing. But then? Even if, after having grasped her and held her fast, he had plunged a knife into her palpitating throat, what would have happened, basically, that was really important? You had only to look at the affairs of life from a certain distance to conclude that they were worth, all of them, only what they were worth: namely nothing, or almost nothing.

When he had passed the side street that, to the left, led to the cemetery and, to the right, beyond the iron bridge, he turned into the old provincial highway that ended at Migliaro, at Migliarino, and, in this direction, as you preferred, either at Ferrara or at Lagosanto and Comacchio, he found himself suddenly up against an isolated building. He stopped a second time. In all these years, strangely, he had never observed it with sufficient attention. It was an old noble palazzo, Venetian in style: of a kind that, just beyond the Po, in the Polesine plain, immediately became rather commonplace. With that handsome two-story façade, so harmonious and pleasing, which gave on the canal, a southern exposure therefore; with the possibility, thanks to the space around it, of planting some trees: yes, this, he thought, this would have been a house to buy, to buy and come to live in! He crossed the street to examine the building more closely. But when he had become fully aware of the state of abandonment in which it stood, the ground-floor entrance replaced by planks carelessly nailed together, the windows without glass and without shutters, the roof half caved in (from below, through a window on the third floor, you could see the sky), he was immediately repelled by it. Disheartened, he imagined the interior, the desolation of the empty rooms, fat sewer rats galloping over the broken floors, the black, gaping mouth of the big fireplace on the piano nobile, from which, on stormy days, gusts of wind must burst and sweep from one end of the drawing room to the other, the fragments of wood—bits of rotten shutters, of doors unhinged for decades—scattered more or less everywhere, and the dust, the cobwebs, the smell, the darkness. No. To restore life to such a corpse would require too much strength: in every sense. Perhaps not even Ulderico would have succeeded, the Ulderico of fifteen years ago, when, still young, he had suddenly decided to burn his bridges, marry an ordinary woman, the first within reach, be baptized, set up house and family in the plain; and disappear, practically speaking.

He went off. But at the first crossing he turned to the left, penetrating again into the tangle of the old town.

One after the other, he followed various streets: tiny alleyways, flanked by little one-story houses of the most ancient part of Codigoro. He met no one. From the slits of the closed shutters filtered the reddish light of the poor families. Only the sound of an occasional radio could be heard.

At the corners, he raised his eyes to read the street signs. He knew it: the day after the Liberation almost all the names of the streets had been changed. Narrow lanes of beaten earth had been pompously dedicated to Carlo Marx, to Federico Engels, to Giuseppe Stalin, to Antonio Gramsci, to Clelia Trotti—the famous elementary-school teacher, a socialist, who died of privations during the winter of '44 right here in Codigoro, in the local prison—to E. Curiel, et cetera. The ceramic signs from before hadn't been removed. They had simply been covered with whitewash. And over the layer of whitewash, with a brush dipped in black paint, the new names had been written by hand. Reading them wasn't easy. Time and bad weather were already erasing them. He spelled out: LO MAR ; ANTON GRAMSCI; E. CURIEL; IUSEPPE TALIN; C E IA ROTTI. He replaced, mentally, one by one, all the missing letters. And he didn't move on until he had finished.

In Via Antonio Labriola, which must have been just behind the square (the convex bulk of the apse of Santa Maria Ausiliatrice, with its bell tower to one side, shut off, over there, the opposite end of the lane), he was attracted by two ground-floor windows, discreetly illuminated. He approached the nearer one, and keeping a bit to one side he looked into the house, through the panes.

He saw a low room, rectangular, medium-sized: a wineshop, evidently. The walls laden with hanging objects, copper pans and casseroles, the sooty fireplace, the two tables, occupied, each one, by four card players with caps or hats on their heads and with a quarter-liter of wine and a glass beside their elbows, allowed no room for doubt on the subject. But the eight players, precisely, so silent, so motionless (the measured gesture with which, from time to time, one of them set a card on the table, only underlined his substantial immobility: his and that of all the others), although they resembled in every detail the customers of the *Bosco Elìceo* and the *Caffè Fetman*, why, there, shut in that room, beyond the window, why did they seem to him so alien, so unapproachable?

He concentrated his attention on the four who occupied the table opposite him. Three of them were workers, probably: all men somewhere between thirty and forty. The one on the right, thin, bony, his profile sharp, his cheeks dark with beard, was perhaps a bricklayer. The one in the middle, facing him, broad-faced, snub-nosed, a black beret pulled crossways on his head, and his hands black with axle grease, a mechanic. The third, on the left, huddled in the rush-bottom chair, his hunched back in a cyclist's jersey, could also be a brick-layer, or perhaps a peasant, one of the kind who tend the livestock. The fourth instead, his back to the window, corpulent, thick-necked, a brown bowler tilted at a carefree angle, wasn't a worker, that was sure, but rather a pensioner of the Reclamation Bureau or the Eridania sugar refinery, or else a small landowner. There wasn't a free chair in the room. Each person, each object, corresponded to a precise function. He felt as if he were standing before a picture in a frame. It was impossible to enter. There was no place, no room for him.

What should he do? Where should he go?

He raised his arm, bared the face of the watch to the light. Ten past seven.

He shifted, holding his chest in, and looked toward the end of the street. There, he said to himself, in church, there he would surely find a bench where he could sit down. He would place himself in a corner, apart, so he wouldn't be noticed in case Ulderico and the children arrived. Crossing the threshold: the only risk would be at that moment. But would it be possible for him to encounter the Cavaglieris just at the door? In any event, he would take great care.

He would never have imagined that the church's interior was so vast. With a single nave, the plain walls whitewashed, and with the floor almost entirely occupied by two ranks of benches divided in the middle by an aisle that led straight to the main altar, it reminded him of a movie house, the empty hall of a movie theater at a time when no film was being shown. There was only the priest, with the altar boy, down near the altar, busy preparing something, and four or five old women huddled here and there on the benches.

At about halfway along the side wall opposite the entrance he noticed a chapel, the only one: a half-dark niche which contained nothing but a large, black crucifix carved in wood. It was there, near the chapel, that he should go and find a seat. If it were necessary, he could withdraw to the back of the chapel. And, on tiptoe, he headed straight in that direction.

As soon as he was seated, he began to stare at the distant, incomprehensible bustling of the priest and the altar boy between the main altar and the sacristy. He didn't feel at ease, however. Having taken off his cap, he felt his head was cold. The proximity of the crucifix, moreover, that black, smoked corpse nailed there, disturbed him, intimidated him.

He yawned. How many people could be seated here, in the church?

He began to count the benches. Beginning with the first row and moving back, he counted up to forty. Each row of benches could comfortably hold about twenty people. Two times four, eight. In other words, there were seats for eight hundred people.

He yawned again. A good half of the benches, especially those up front, those closest to the main altar, bore, on them, a little white plate. He could imagine the family names printed on those plates: the usual Callegari, Callegarini, Benazzi, Tagliati, Putinati, Pimpinati, Borgatti, Fellitti, Mingozzi, Bottoni, et cetera: the same, more or less, that you encountered in the country, among the hired hands and the humblest workmen.

And Cavaglieri? Would they have one too, their private pew in the church? It was almost worth going over to see.

He realized his foot was pressing on something. He looked down. Some paper. It looked like a newspaper.

He bent down. He picked it up. He straightened his back again.

It wasn't a newspaper: it was a little pamphlet of Catholic propaganda. On the front page there was only a woodcut, heavily inked. It depicted a hand in the act of pressing some ripe olives from a bough. Rough, with enormous nails, the knotty fingers were dripping oil. The whole picture was surmounted by a headline in capital letters, widely spaced, saying: TAKE NO THOUGHT FOR THE MORROW.

He opened the sheet, unfolding it.

There was a great deal of matter, inside, to read. To invite the reader's attention, the type face changed constantly. The layout, too, changed every now and then. Sometimes a full line was suddenly followed by short lines, arranged in one column, in the center, as if they were the verses of a poem.

"Have you ever examined a mole carefully?" he read, starting at the top line, at the left, and half closing his eyelids to decipher the tiny italic letters of the first words.

"Its forepaws are in the form of a shovel: with them, it digs the earth in front of itself, as you would do with a spoon. The rear paws serve to push the body forward. The head resembles a wedge, and the nose is like a pointed chisel; but both are made in such a way that they don't break. The animal's tiny eyes are almost entirely hidden in its fur, and so are its ears.

"Just think: did it become this way on its own, adapting its body to its underground way of life? And why have other animals, which live in the same conditions, adapted themselves differently? The answer, of course, is God. But can a God who is infinitely great bother about such small, unimportant creatures?

"Refuse to listen to that voice, the voice of atheistic materialism! Look instead at everything that surrounds you. See it with the clear, good eye of a child of God. And then you will understand St. Augustine, who tells us: 'God cares for each creature as if it were the only one in the world, and he cares for all creatures as if they were one.'

"There are different ways of caring, however.

"You take care of your shoes, of your hunting dog and of your parakeet, of the pot of geraniums on your window sill, of your radio, your bicycle; but, when it comes to your little girl: 'Watch out! Don't fall!' 'This draft isn't good for you!' 'Are you hungry?' 'I must run and see why she's crying . . .'; and you press her to your heart and dry her tears.

"God, among all His creatures, takes special care of mankind, which He loves with a father's heart.

"After having created, for your use, the air, the sun, fruit, stones to build your house, the hides and the wool of animals to clothe you, and grass and flowers to give you pleasure, He bends down to you and can even hear the beating of your heart, which He soothes with the security He gives your life.

"He says to you: Be not solicitous for your life, what you shall eat, or what you shall drink. Behold the birds of the air, for they neither sow, nor do they reap, nor gather into barns; and your heavenly Father feedeth them. Are not you of much more value than they? And for raiment why are you solicitous? Consider the lilies of the field, how they grow: they labor not, neither do they spin. But I say unto you, that not even Solomon in all his glory was arrayed as one of these. . . .

"Wherefore, if God so clothe the grass of the field, which today is and tomorrow is cast into the oven, shall He not much more clothe you! He provides always for your true welfare, be sure of that, even when things aren't going just as you would like."

He had reached the end of the page: the third.

"The parakeet?" he thought. "What does a parakeet have to do with any of this?"

He turned to the last page. It was blank. There was nothing else to read.

III

He came out by the same little side door through which he had entered. And almost at once, after only a few steps along the darkness of the malodorous little alley that flanked the church, he found himself in the square, at the edge of the paved area in front of the church's main entrance.

Once again he stopped.

Opening gradually like a cup, or a funnel, the square stretched out before him in all its vast expanse. On the right, in the foreground, the murky wing of the former Casa del Fascio. On the left, just as high but set farther back, the I.N.A. building with its dozens of brilliantly lighted windows. In the rear, at a distance which seemed enormous to him, so enormous that the thought of covering it on foot filled him with weariness, with a boundless ennui, there were three sources of light: two were the facing cafés, *Fetman* and *Moccia*, with an equally dull yellow glow, and then the light of a shop window of which he had just then become aware, close, practically speaking, on his right, to the low central building of the Labor Council, and with the same dazzling white, vivid glare, like an industrial plant in full activity, as that which poured in torrents from the I.N.A. building. No fog. On the contrary: during that last half-hour, the atmosphere had actually turned crystalline. Clear as it had become, it enabled him to distinguish in every detail not only the Monument to the Dead, in the middle of the square, but also, behind it, the tiny, opaque, bug carapace of the Aprilia's roof. He sniffed the air. In his nostrils had remained the odors of urine and incense. With those, however, and with the usual odor of the valleys, a new smell was mingling: a burning. Roast chestnuts. He looked around, seeking the humble iron brazier, filled with charcoal, which was producing the aroma somewhere nearby. But he looked in vain. Who could tell where it was coming from?

He went off.

He moved slowly, allowing his legs to carry him toward the center of the square, and meanwhile the space around him, and everything included within it, the Monument to the Dead, the former Casa del Fascio, the I.N.A. building, each thing gradually took on a different aspect, was slowly modified. The Aprilia itself was changing its appearance. It was no longer the little shell it had been a moment before, flattened against the ground. He could already see its double rear window, in trapezoidal segments. And in a moment, white against a black ground, it would be possible to read the number on his license plate preceded by the letters FE.

He headed straight for the *Caffè Fetman*. But when he had covered about three-quarters of the distance, having seen a little group of customers come out of the place and stop, then, to chat on the sidewalk in front of the door (there were four men, all in cloaks: and they seemed, too, to be carefully examining the Aprilia, talking about it together), rather than have to climb into the car before their eyes, he preferred to turn right, toward the bright window beside the Labor Council. He had long since realized what the place was: it was the taxidermist's shop Bellagamba had mentioned to him.

But that didn't matter. Without feeling, at the idea, the slightest revulsion, he continued to allow his legs, one step after the other, to lead him there, perhaps a yard away from the great slab of glass.

He stopped abruptly, fascinated.

Hunting guns, cartridge belts pregnant with ammunition, fishing rods, nets, little mirrors for larks, decoys, rubber boots, woolen clothing, or homespun, or corduroy, as well as, of course, stuffed animals, birds, most of them, but there was also a fox, a marten, a few squirrels, some turtles: heaped high with objects arranged in what was only apparently disorder, the window gleamed before him like a little, sun-filled universe to itself, adjacent but unattainable. He knew: there was the glass, between them, to achieve this. And since the glass, though so clean it was almost invisible, reflected something of his own image (barely a shadow, true, but still irksome), in order to erase it completely, this faint residual shade, and to give himself the illusion that the glass itself didn't exist, he moved closer, until he was almost touching the window with his forehead, feeling it graze his face with a cold even colder than the evening air.

Beyond the glass: silence, absolute stillness, peace.

One by one, he looked at the stuffed animals, magnificent, all of them, in their death, more alive than if they were alive.

The fox, for example, which occupied, horizontally, the center of the window between two huge rubber boots, erect and paired, and a half-opened shotgun, turned its grinning muzzle to one side as if, at that very moment, it had just finished moving; and from its yellow eyes, full of hatred, from its white teeth, its red, bright jaws, its tawny fur, rich and shiny, from its puffed up, disproportionate tail, burst an overwhelming, almost insolent health, saved as if by enchantment from any possible harm, of today or tomorrow. The squirrels, too, placed where you would least have expected to find them (there was one who showed only its little head from inside a leather game bag), though motionless, still managed to express not only a malicious grace, an agility, their natural, Walt-Disney-gnomes' gaiety, but something else, something more, connected in some way with their being there, in safety, and forever, behind the great glass wall. In the violent, converging light of the bulbs, the tiny black pinheads of their eyes shone joyously, feverishly, demoniacal in their wisdom and their irony.

It was the birds, however, on which his eyes would never have tired of gazing.

The ducks, at least a dozen, filled in a compact group the proscenium of the little theater: so close you thought you could touch them, and calm, finally, not frightened, not forced to keep aloft, suspended on their short, fluttering wings, in the mobile and treacherous air. The birds of prey, instead, except for an eagle owl, perched, up above, in a central and dominating position, were farther back, lined along a kind of shelf which ran all around the sides and across the rear of the window. Reading the little brass plates at the base of the fake-ebony pedestals on each of which a bird stood erect, he recognized, one by one, a kestrel, a buzzard, a peregrine falcon, an osprey, a sparrow hawk. . . . In any case, the birds, too, were alive, with a life that no longer ran any risk of deteriorating; polished to a high gloss; but made beautiful, above all, surely more beautiful, and by a great deal, than when they were breathing and the blood ran swiftly through their veins: only he, perhaps, he thought, was able really to *understand* it, the perfection of this beauty of theirs, final and imperishable, to appreciate it fully.

At one point, to catch better the touch of green in the feathers of a mallard, he was forced to step back a few inches. And immediately, for the second time, he glimpsed, reflected in the glass, the outline of his own face.

He tried then to look at himself as he had looked at himself that same morning, in the bathroom mirror. And as he was rediscovering, precisely, before him, under the fur cap, the same features of every wakening —the bald forehead, the three horizontal lines that crossed it from temple to temple, the long and fleshy nose, the heavy, weary eyelids, the flabby and almost womanish lips, the hole in the chin, the wan cheeks, smudged by his beard—but such, still, as to seem veiled to him, removed, as if just a few hours had been enough to scatter over those features the dust of years and years, he felt slowly approaching, within him, vague as yet, but rich in mysterious promises, a secret thought that would free him, save him.

IV

If he had only had to imagine himself dead in order
to feel overwhelmed by a sudden wave of happiness, he
reasoned inwardly, smiling, then why not kill himself?
And why not do it as soon as possible? No: he would do
it that very night, in his bedroom, with the Browning or
with the Krupp. And he already knew how.

He was driving along the road to Ferrara in the cold,
clear night, illuminated by the moon.

Just before the Eridania refinery and the Reclamation Bureau he had stopped at an A.G.I.P. station to buy
five hundred lire's worth of gas and to have them clean
the windshield; and now, in the car, after having decided what he had decided, it was even easier for him to
identify with the stuffed animals in Cimini's shop in
Codigoro. Every now and then he shook his head. How
stupid it became, life, this much-vaunted life, how ri-
diculous and grotesque, he said to himself, when you
saw it from inside the window of a taxidermist's! And
how well he felt, immediately, at the very thought of
giving up all that monotonous round of eating and
defecating, of drinking and urinating, of sleeping and
waking up, of moving about and standing still, of
which life consisted! For the first time, perhaps, since
he had come into the world, he was thinking of the
dead without fear. Only they, the dead, counted for
something, existed truly. It took them a couple of years
to be reduced to pure skeletons: he had read this somewhere. After which they changed no more, never again.

Clean, hard, beautiful, they had by then become like precious stones, like the noble metals. Unchangeable, and therefore eternal.

The closer he came to Ferrara, all the same, the more his reflections grew jolly, light, at times even frivolous. He kept bursting into laughter.

The rapid glimpse of La Montina on the left of the road, beyond the Volano Po, had reminded him of Nives. And at once he had begun thinking, with amusement, of what, in a month's time, or a month and a half, would happen at La Montina when she, Nives, turned up there in person for a first contact with the property and with her underlings. He could see it all with extreme precision: the lordly frown of the widow and heiress, the fastidious pursing of her lips, concerned with expressing herself in the best possible Italian, the bowing and scraping of Benazzi the manager, hopeful of being kept on in his job, the hats in the hands of the workers and the livestock men, now disposed, in view of the trend politics was taking, to pass a huge sponge over the recent past, their faces half sly, half devoted and contrite. But, as he thought of it—and he chuckled, kindly—would Nives come alone to La Montina, or would she be driven there in the Aprilia by the faithful Prearo? That there was something up between the two of them, and had been for some time, only he, with his inveterate tendency to see nothing that might endanger his calm, only he had been able not to know. So then, why not? In view of the rather solemn occasion, it was probable that the excellent bookkeeper would, for once, serve also as chauffeur, remaining, during the whole proprietary inspection, slightly to one side, respectfully *à côté*. Oh, the scene would be something to enjoy, from beginning to end, and it was a shame he had to miss it. But for that matter: wasn't there enough reason for satisfaction in his being able to foresee it in his imagination, and in the fact that he, her husband after all, was arranging for it really to happen?

He was so detached from himself and from the world, now, so at ease and peaceful, that a little farther on, at the gates of Tresigallo, the name of the town, written in big letters on the outside wall of a house at the edge of the settlement, struck him as if his eyes had never noticed it before then. Tresigallo. What sort of origin could it have had, a name like that? That same evening he must remind himself to look it up in Frizzi or in the Treccani encyclopedia. Perhaps he could garner some information on this matter.

But meanwhile he was slowly crossing the town, which was also dark, deserted. He remembered clearly: about fifteen years ago, around '30, the Fascist government had suddenly decided to transform this little agricultural center, one of the smallest and most insignificant of the province, into a kind of Littoria, another Fascist model village in the heart of the Ferrara farmland, to use the words that they used in those days: and there, in fact, the car's headlights discovered a huge building faced with marble on the order of the Casa del Fascio in Codigoro, and there, a broad endless square with, in its center, high above the plinth of black basalt that supported it, a statue of Roman travertine, and farther on an industrial building that resembled the new railroad station in Florence, and created, as a perfectly legible inscription on the top of the entrance gate still announced, for the processing of hemp and its by-products. It was clear: nowadays, none of this was good for anything any more. The big building with its imperial air; the statue of the gladiator with his bare, muscular behind, symbolizing no doubt Fascism On the March; the plant designed for making "national" cloth: under the moon, the whole complex was revealed as meaningless, a mere stage setting; and the life of the village seemed more than ever restricted to the little circle of peasant houses of the past, grouped off to one side around the old parish church. He drove out of the other end of the settlement. "Bon voyage," he muttered, accelerating along the broad, tree-lined road that led straight to Ferrara. In the course of the day, this was the second time he had expressed a bon voyage wish. This morning, to those poor ducks; now to Tresigallo. Again he had to laugh. Still it was only right, after all. After all, Tresigallo had a tomorrow before itself. Though on a narrower gauge, the village continued to move, to go forward. Whereas he, on the contrary (and he thought this without a shadow of sadness, indeed with a kind of calm merriment), where was he going, with his car?

The arches of Corso Giovecca loomed up before his hood when it was exactly twenty past nine. Before leaving Codigoro he had remembered to call home. From the familiar booth in the *Caffè Fetman* he had exchanged a few words with Elsa, the cook: only to say that he was leaving, that he expected to arrive in about fifty minutes, and would she please call Romeo, downstairs, and tell him to open the main gate ahead of time. He was now right on schedule. Had Elsa, then, carried out his instructions? Considering the late hour and the supper she had to prepare, perhaps not, she had probably forgotten them. In a moment, anyway, he would know. If the gates were closed, no harm done: he would blow the horn a couple of times.

The moon illuminated Via Montebello for all its length: from the crossing at Corso Giovecca all the way down, in the distance, to the massive arch of grayish granite set at the entrance to the Jewish cemetery. Via Mentana, conversely, was almost in darkness. As soon as he had turned the corner, he flashed on his bright lights for a moment. The gate was wide open. In front of it, standing at the edge of the sidewalk, with his cap on his head, the beige wool scarf wrapped around his neck, his hands deep in the pockets of his trousers, Romeo was calmly waiting.

He slowed down; he cast a glance in the rear-view mirror; he shifted to the other side, the left side, of the street, put out his flipper; swung all around to the right. Then, accelerating again, he drove straight through the gates and stopped at his usual place, in the middle of the portico.

He waited until Romeo had shut the gates and until his old, parchmenty face was framed, cautiously, in the window, beyond the glass. Why didn't the Signor Avvocato make up his mind to get out of the car? Barely concealed, his amazement was comical and at the same time moving.

He rolled the window down halfway.

"Open the inner gate for me, please," he said calmly, pointing ahead.

The man's eyes widened.

"You want to leave the car out in the courtyard?" he asked, in his slow Italian used on state occasions.

"Yes," he smiled. "It doesn't seem so cold to me, after all."

"Do you have much stuff to take out?"

He understood what Romeo meant: the booty of the hunt. The old man didn't believe there was any, though. The thin, purplish lips were stretched in a furtive grin.

"No, not at all. I didn't shoot a thing."

Through the windshield he saw the man head for the gate. It was obvious that he disapproved. It could be deduced from the way his back was bent, more accentuated than usual, as he fumbled to open the gate. What with one thing and another, he would have to make a bit more work for Romeo in a little while. So now he must try to be kind, to keep him in a good humor.

He drove the car out into the courtyard.

"And how is your daughter getting on?" he asked, when he had stepped out. "Did she come to see you this afternoon?"

Yes, she had come, Romeo confirmed. They had both turned up together: she and the husband.

He added nothing further and twisted his mouth. Probably he had had to produce some money, he thought. But, in any case, what could he do about it? To suggest reimbursing Romeo was out of the question: apart from the fact that he had only a few hundred lire, and it was too difficult to broach the subject. And as far as speaking to the son-in-law went, that William, he just didn't feel he could promise that. To promise it, knowing he couldn't keep the promise, would have been, on his part, dishonest. Dishonest and stupid.

He walked briskly up the main staircase, with the Browning and the Krupp hanging each from one shoulder. But when he had reached the upper floor, in the hall, he stopped. From the little dining room next door, he had clearly heard Nives's whining voice. Since they were already at table, perhaps the best thing for him to do was to show himself at once. And afterwards, perhaps, he could go for a moment into the bedroom, to wash his face and hands.

He walked across the polished, creaking parquet, opened the double door a crack, and stuck his head between its two leaves.

"I'm here," he said, as Lilla, his mother's French poodle, came out with her usual little stifled bark. "Hello."

He had taken them by surprise.

Nives and his mother at either end of the table, Rory and Prearo in the middle, one opposite the other: they all looked at him, their eyes filled with wonder, all as motionless as statues. Odd. Odd and funny. Could Elsa, who had, after all, told Romeo, have neglected to inform Nives at least of his phone call? No, it wasn't possible: also considering that, beside Rory, on her right, a fifth place had been set. . . .

He took a step forward.

"Good evening," Prearo murmured, half rising from his chair and twisting his sweaty face around.

"Please, don't get up."

"Aren't you going to sit down?" Nives complained. "Come on in, it's late."

At that very moment Elsa was coming through the door opposite, which led to the pantry and the kitchen. In both hands she was holding the oval dish of boiled turkey loaf; and she too, seeing him, stopped abruptly.

He took them all in, with a single circular glance:

Nives, Rory, his mother with the curly little black dog huddled on a chair beside her, Prearo, Elsa. He felt incredibly rich, generous, disposed to give: in the grip of a kind of intoxication. And yet he knew, oh how well he knew. It would have sufficed for him to think, for that matter, of surviving just one more day, and the happiness that for an hour he had borne within him, locked inside him like a treasure, would dissolve at once, and he would again feel toward his daughter, sitting there, staring at him over the edge of her spoon with her beautiful eyes of a dark, wild blue, the usual, bitter sense of foreignness, almost of revulsion, which had always prevented him from considering her his own, from loving her. So then, he said to himself, it was only by dying that he could love her, love Rory! And she? Would she remember him, when she was grown up, her father? His physical appearance? Almost certainly not. He wished this for her freely, anyhow: with all his heart. At the point he had reached, this was the only gift he was capable of giving her.

"I'm going to my room for a moment," he said.

V

He had been the first to believe that, in a moment, he would go back there. But when he had left the dining room, and had begun to walk down the long L-shaped hall which led from the vestibule to his room, he understood suddenly that he wouldn't show himself again, not even to announce that he had decided to skip supper. To be alone, undress, think. Prepare himself. Nothing else was pressing; he desired nothing else.

He went into the bedroom; he turned on the overhead light; he took off the cartridge belt, setting it on a chair; he slipped the two guns from his shoulders and went to prop them against the wall, beside the glass case; he removed his jacket, hanging it on the clothes-stand; he sat down on the edge of the bed, leaned over to undo the laces of his boots; he stood up again; he turned on the lamp on the night table; he turned off the overhead light; finally he lay down, his hands clasped behind his head. And he was still lying in that position, staring at the darkened ceiling, all filled with the sense of extraordinary well-being that lying again on his bed gave him, stretched out supine on his own bed, when he heard a knock at the door.

"Come in," he said.

It was Elsa: he could tell by the odor, a mingled smell of kitchen and soap.

"What is it?" he asked, without moving, and lowering his eyelids.

The broth with rice was becoming cold, the girl answered. If the Signor Avvocato didn't come promptly, afterwards, if it was heated up a second time, it wouldn't be so good.

He knew where she was: just inside the threshold, leaning on the door handle with her hand, the fingers swollen and chapped, but she was pleasant, not disagreeable.

"No, I'm not coming," he answered. "I'm not hungry. Tell the Signora."

He half pulled himself up, leaning on one elbow, and turned to smile at her.

"And besides," he added, "I'm too tired."

In the penumbra, with the lamplight that rose from below to graze her cheeks bursting with health, he saw her blush. Where was it she came from? Ah yes: from Chioggia, or rather from Sottomarina di Chioggia. Blonde, pink, sturdy, with pale blue eyes, too, like Irma Manzoli, she was constantly blushing; and he had always liked women who blushed easily.

"Do you need anything?" she asked him.

He was about to say no. But something occurred to him. What if there was no string in the house? That would be a fine fix. To do it, to shoot himself, he would absolutely need some.

He raised a finger.

"Do you have any string in there, in the kitchen?"

"String?"

Poor girl. She was right to look at him with that expression, of wonder and irony.

"Before going to sleep," he explained, "I'd like to clean up the guns a bit."

"I think so. But how long does it have to be?"

"Five or six feet is enough."

"I'll go and look."

"Thank you," and again he smiled. "Thanks a lot."

When he had heard the door close, he stood up, slipped the watch from his wrist, set it on the table, and went into the bathroom.

First of all he turned on the faucets of the tub, leaning over them to adjust the temperature of the water carefully. And gradually as he undressed (he knew what he wanted: he would undress, wash himself carefully, shave; later he would even try to defecate), gradually as he took off the pullovers, the flannel shirt, the undershirt, and then, afterwards, the heavy wool stockings, the light socks, the corduroy pants, the long woolen underwear, the shorts, he thought only of how he would manage to shoot himself, forcing himself to define, in advance, with precision, every detail of the operation.

In the country—he had heard it told many times— the peasants generally did it this way: they placed the gun on the floor, its butt, and then, holding the barrel firmly in their hands, they pressed the trigger with their toe. But he would do it in a different fashion. He would take the string, tie one end to the trigger and the other to something solid, fixed, perhaps one of the faucets of the tub. Then, having made himself comfortable, seated, he would pull the barrel toward him. No, he said to himself, the string was decidedly a good trick, a magnificent invention. Remaining seated, he could shoot himself in the chest, in the throat, in the mouth, in the center of his forehead: wherever he preferred. And, in the bathroom, moreover, it didn't matter much if he stained the floor.

He stepped over the edge of the tub, turned off both faucets, and lay down in the tepid water.

The only point that was still to be settled, he went on thinking, and the sudden silence helped him, was, if anything, the weapon. Which would he use? The Browning or the Krupp? But as he asked himself this question he already knew that he would leave the Browning alone, he would take care not to use it. The Krupp was better, he reasoned. Its double barrels were much more sure. With the double-barreled gun, the risk of remaining there, half alive, his blood draining slowly away, became slight. If he was able to calculate accurately the lengths of the string, one for each trigger, he would receive two shots at once: at the same moment. He wouldn't be aware of a thing.

He soaped himself from head to foot; he rinsed himself off again; he stepped out of the tub; he dried himself; shaved; patted his face with a bit of cologne, combed his hair carefully, using brilliantine, comb and brush. Finally, having put on his pajamas and the camel-colored wool robe, putting his feet into his slippers, he went back to the bedroom.

Elsa had brought the string. She had brought a whole ball, leaving it clearly in sight, in the center of the bed. He took the ball in his hand, examined it. Excellent. The string was fine: for small packages, but strong, the most suitable. The knots, with this string, would come out perfectly.

He set the ball on the night table next to the Vacheron-Constantin and the Jaeger, then he lay on the bed again, on top of the blankets, his hands clasped behind his head as before. He would leave nothing written. Not even a line. What was the use? He had no debts to pay or credits to collect. And, as for the cemetery, he could rest assured on that score. Prearo had regularly paid the annual dues to the Jewish community, absolutely regularly: in his name and in his mother's. No one, then, could raise any objections. The president of the community himself, that Cohen, who had cut him after his marriage to Nives, and had never spoken to him since, would find his hands tied.

He lay there, thinking still.

Toward midnight he got out of bed, went to the door, opened it, and stepped into the hall.

Not always, true, but often, he went to visit his mother more or less at this hour: whether he had just come home from outside, or whether, after supper, he had retired to his room to read the newspapers in peace or to do some accounts. It was an old habit, very old. But for this very reason it might well be that his mother, perhaps concerned at not seeing him arrive, could happen into his room at two or three o'clock: when he would most need to be alone, to be undisturbed.

He walked along the hall, crossed the vestibule, the dining room, and the two drawing rooms after it, one opening into the other, which for about ten years had no longer been heated, and were now permanently destined to be places for storing things. He moved from one end of the apartment to the other, in short, opening and closing doors, turning lights on and off, not caring if he made the parquet floors creak. If Nives from her room, or Elsa from her little closet next to the kitchen, were to hear him go by, so much the better. Much better that this night should seem, also to them, absolutely normal, not different, in any way, from so many others.

VI

His inner joy gave impetus to his weary legs, measure and precision to his movements, calm to the beating of his heart. It was really a treasure, what he bore within himself. Immense, yes, inexhaustible; but yet to be kept secret, hidden from any person in the world. All his happiness, all his peace stemmed from the certainty that he was its sole owner.

Made out of a smallish room that from time immemorial—the time of his grandfather Eliseo and his grandmother Vittoria—had been used only for billiards, his mother's bedroom was the last room of the apartment, the most distant. But when he had walked through the vast, icy darkness of the second of the two former drawing rooms, full of dark, shapeless presences, there at last was the door. He lowered the handle and opened it a crack.

"May I come in?" he said, as usual.

"Oh, it's you!" he heard, in reply, the well-known voice, querulous and shaky.

He entered, shut the door after him, and advanced in the sudden warmth toward the bed placed at the other end of the room. He sat down beside it and reached out to give a pat to Lilla, who, having performed her brief, innocuous, ritual growl, had promptly curled up again at her mistress' side, against her hip. He behaved, in other words, as he did each time, repeating the familiar actions, the same movements, and preparing to say and hear the same words as always.

But for once he was happy; and from the very beginning his mother, too, was infected with his happiness.

Instead of starting with the customary complaints, of which, generally, Nives had to bear the brunt, she looked at him, with satisfaction, in silence.

"Aren't we handsome," she said, finally.

"Me? Handsome?" he parried. "Go on."

"Yes, yes, let your Mamma tell you! You ought to go out hunting more often. Being out in the sun, in the wind, getting a bit of fresh air every now and then as in the old days, would do you good, I'm sure of that. If you could just see how well you look."

"Yes, maybe you're right," he said, bowing his head. "I really could use it."

"Good for you," she smiled. "I noticed right away, the minute you came home, that your whole expression was different. But why . . . ," she went on, still smiling and speaking in a low voice, "why wouldn't you eat anything, not even a little bowl of soup? It was very good."

"I'm sure it was. The fact is that today I had dinner very late. So I wasn't hungry."

"Too bad. Your wife insisted on making the meat loaf herself, but I have to admit that she's finally learned how. Even that was very good. . . . And where did you go to eat today?"

He told her where.

"Goodness knows what sort of rubbish you ate there!" she exclaimed, with a grimace of disgust. "I hope it doesn't do you any harm. But did the underwear, at least, keep you warm and dry?"

As he was saying yes, the woolen underwear had been providential, and telling her, then, calmly, what he had eaten for dinner, he was observing her. In bed,

174

with the two linen pillows behind her back, with that pretty crocheted bed jacket of blue wool that covered her shoulders and her chest, but clean, above all, the soft cottony hair hardly whiter than the frail parchment of her face, she, too, was beautiful, very beautiful. Perfect.

"You're very beautiful, too," he said. "Congratulations."

She burst out laughing. Childishly flattered, she sank back in the pillows, clasped her gnarled little hands, covered with veins, and lowered her eyelids. How old was she? he wondered. She must be about eighty; almost twice his age, then. But it was also true that her arteriosclerosis was helping her become a child again: even more of a child than Rory.

When she reopened her eyes, she wanted to know how the hunting had gone.

"You didn't shoot anything, I imagine," she said.

She had assumed a disillusioned manner and anxious at the same time: as if she asked for nothing more than to be contradicted. Why not satisfy her? She wanted to be told a fairy tale, and he would tell her one. Gladly.

He answered that she was mistaken, he had brought down about forty birds, ducks and coots. Only instead of bringing them home, he had preferred to give them away. He had made a present of them all to Ulderico.

It took her a while to understand.

"Ulderico who?" she asked.

She nodded her head toward Via Montebello, then added, lowering her voice:

"*Cavaglieri?*"

He nodded.

He waited until she had recovered from her amazement, until she could reorganize her memory. Yes, Ulderico, he confirmed. Since, recently, they had spoken to each other a couple of times on the phone, and Ulderico had been so kind, as he was going by Codigoro, he had decided to visit him.

She was paying close attention, now: as if she had become twenty years younger.

"At his house?" she whispered.

"Yes, at his house."

"And where is their house? In the country?"

"No, in the town. Right on the square."

"Did you see his wife, too?"

"His wife and the children."

"Children! How many have they produced?"

He held up his fingers.

"Six!" his mother exclaimed at this point, clapping her hands. "Good Lord, what a tribe!"

"And the wife . . . ," she went on, after a pause, her voice again stifled, and her forehead frowning in her effort to remember, ". . . what's the wife like? Did you talk with her?"

"Of course. I telephoned, I went there, they gave me a nice cup of tea. . . . They even wanted me to stay to supper."

He saw her shake her head, heaving a deep sigh, as she sank back again on the pillows. Her brown eyes, always a bit too moist, had filled with tears. What was she thinking about? What had come over her? No sadness, for God's sake.

To distract her, he told her then about the children. The girls, both of them, were big now. Of the four boys, all handsome and likable, three, while he was there, had started playing football in the entrance hall.

"I can just imagine the racket!" his mother laughed, still in tears.

"Yes, it was noisy."

"And what are their names, poor things?"

"Oh, I don't know. Clementina, Tonino . . . or Tanino, I didn't catch it. There's one named Andrea, too."

Here they were interrupted by Lilla, who, springing suddenly to her feet, had started barking. Her ear was very sensitive, he had noticed that already in the past. Anything, a truck passing by from Corso Giovecca, for example, was enough to make her pop up like a spring and protest.

"Down!" his mother scolded her. "Lie down, silly, and go to sleep!"

When she had made sure that the dog was sleeping again, she seemed to have suddenly forgotten everything they had said until then.

Now she began talking, uninterruptedly, as was her custom: about Lilla, so smart, she said, that if one fine day the dog started to say "Mamma" only those who didn't know her would be surprised; and about Nives, so clever, of course, with a head on her shoulders, a real worker, a toiler actually, but often a bit curt—how to put it?—a bit rustic; and about the bookkeeper Prearo, who this very evening, at table, had announced that political matters were taking a turn for the better, and this moreover was in perfect accord with the great peace that for some time now she had also felt around her, a calm very similar, she felt, to that period she had spent in Fiesole, in the convent, when the Germans were here; and about Rory, who, poor child, that very noon had slipped a little Christmas wish under her napkin, so prettily written, neat and well expressed, and so affectionate; and about a water pipe that leaked more every day, and he should keep after Romeo until he made up his mind to have a look at it; and about a telephone call she had received at five o'clock from her old friend Carmen Scutellari, one of the Scutellari family of Via Terranuova, a phone call that had ended with their promising to visit each other in the next few days, and so on. It was a steady flow of softly spoken words, a kind of chirping: which ended, after no less than twenty minutes, with yet another sigh and a "hmph," definitely satisfied, blissful.

For her, too, everything came out right, he thought, as he started to get up. For the little that was left for her to live, everything would come out right. Whatever happened.

He leaned over to kiss her temple.

"Good night," he said.

"Yes, dear. Good night to you, too."

He turned his back to her, crossed the room, and reached the door.

With his hand on the knob, he stopped and looked at her. Surrounded by all that was most hers and most personal, her idolized little dog almost in physical contact, and then the family photographs, the arms of the House of Savoy, framed in silver, the varicolored medicine bottles, the leather spectacles case, the tiny gilded parallelopiped of her Zenith alarm clock, the books on one shelf, the latest bound collections of *Vie d'Italia* on another shelf, the *Giornale dell'Emilia* lying on a green silk quilt, at the same level with the tiny clump of black fur that was Lilla, et cetera et cetera, she was still smiling at him. White, over there, enclosed in her cocoon of light . . .

"Good night," he repeated.

"Good night, dear Edgardo."